Close

D1638179

Close

& Other Stories
by
James Robertson

with illustrations by
Simon Manfield

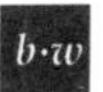

B+W PUBLISHING • EDINBURGH

B+W PUBLISHING • 7 SCIENNES • EDINBURGH • EH9 1NH

First published 1991
by B+W Publishing
© James Robertson 1991
All rights reserved.
No part of this publication may be
reproduced, or transmitted, in any form
or by any means without the prior
permission of B+W Publishing.
ISBN 1 873631 00 6

*The publisher acknowledges subsidy
from the Scottish Arts Council towards
the publication of this volume.*

*The author would like to thank Iain Crichton Smith for
permission to quote from his poem 'Old Woman'.*

*A version of 'Right Side of the Curtain' has previously
appeared in Radical Scotland.*

British Library Cataloguing In Publication Data
A catalogue record for this book is available from the British Library

Printed by Billings of Worcester

23/24 LM £3

Clos

1

Border

He woke at five o'clock as the train was passing through a stretch of what he guessed was Northumberland. The light was coming up, so that the land was crossed and overlaid with beautiful eerie shades. The carriage was only a quarter full - people, mostly young like himself, prepared to forego comfort for the cheap overnight fare, curled up defensively on the seats, slumped in angular conflict with the seats, seemingly at prayer across the tables between the seats. The train was racing, but its noise had settled into the background during the night and it was the light that woke him.

He stretched his legs against the ache of a poor sleep that lay in the hollows of his knees. His hair lay lank on his head. His face when he rubbed his eyes felt greasy. His shirt smelt, though not too bad. His mouth, also, tasted like an unchanged shirt.

He could have done with a drink to freshen his mouth but thought the buffet was surely closed. An empty lemonade can lay crushed on its side on the table in front of him. Also the plastic wrappings from a plastic-tasting sandwich. He could have done with a piss too but he didn't want to get up. Anyway, the train was possibly about to arrive at Berwick station where he would have to wait before flushing the toilet and by waiting he might miss the border.

Not that it was important and yet certainly it was important. It had always been important and now it was more so. Not to everybody. It depended on how you looked at it. Whether or not you could see it. And what it meant if you did. And not just the signpost that told you. That least of all. And yet you needed the signpost to tell you, otherwise you could never be sure and your imagination might play tricks on you. You needed to be sure and yet the signpost didn't matter because the border would still be there even if they took the signpost down. As one day they maybe would.

He remembered a boy. A small boy with his face pressed to the window. The glass feeling on his nose, damp but not damp, and on the other side of the glass dirty rain dribbles tracking across his view. You could look at the glass, the drops of rain, or you could look through them. To the grey, the dull grey outside and the flashes of dull greens and browns as the train picked up speed.

"Soon," said the boy's father. "Any minute."

The boy shifted. His shoulder was aching, but he could not sit back now. He was afraid to blink. His eyes smarted from refusing to blink, as though the wind rushing outside the train were inside, in the carriage. He knew without looking that his mother opposite was trying to sleep, head tilted on rigid neck against the motion of the train, mouth taut and thin. How could she sleep like that? Her eyes had flickered open at Berwick and closed again. She didn't care. She would miss it, but she didn't care.

The boy cared. Ever since Newcastle he had stared at the greyness, the flashing greens and browns. His geography wasn't that good, and he couldn't remember the order of the stations ahead or the distances between them. He knew what was behind: London, where his uncle stayed in a house bigger than theirs; Peterborough, York, Darlington. Ahead, eventually, Edinburgh. But before eventually?

He didn't want to ask his father because his father would expect him to know, so he martyred himself by watching the English land fly by. He thought of reivers and other marauders, and somewhere out there - miles out there - was a place called Otterburn where a battle had been fought centuries ago. It was one of many battles that were mentioned in a book of Scottish history he had. Sometimes he went through the pages of the book counting up the victories and defeats and draws for each side, but the result was always the same. He thought there might be other battles not mentioned in that book that might level the scores. He fought them.

His father must have known what he was looking for but he didn't explain. He didn't say, "Relax. It's not till after Berwick." But after Berwick he said, "Soon. Any minute."

The young man heard these words in his own head. He smiled at them kindly. But in spite of this calm, his heart was beating quite fast now, as the train slowed and stopped. It was in expectation of seeing an invisible line. That was the magic of it. There was a time - a vague time between then and now - when he had doubted its existence. Now he was sure, as sure as the boy had always been. It did not divide people or land. It announced a change: "All pass through me: I pass through all, but they do not know it."

There were ways by road that could be taken. There was a road past Otterburn and one past Solway Moss and another past Flodden, but not having a car he never went these ways. They were not what it was about. They were about mud and old armour. What it was really about was something else, something more.

You could stop a car at these places. You could go off the main road and stop and think about the past. Not *your* past, but *the* . . . . Border history. You could almost touch the past: a monument - you could reach out and touch it. A stone moment - almost the past, but never quite. But the past touched everybody, whether they reached out or not.

By road at Coldstream the border flowed under you. On the train you could think up to it, the border, and beyond it; you could think on either side of it. But itself, it was a moment, a flash through the streaming window. A moment, and change.

The boy's uncle was his father's brother. He had gone to work in London before the boy was born. He was settled there. They stayed for a week and used the big house as a base to see the sights. In the evenings the boy listened to his father and his uncle talking, each with a dram in their big knots of hands. His uncle was a big friendly distant man. When he spoke of home he meant Scotland but it did not sound like the same place. Before very long the boy realised why this was.

The train moved out of Berwick. "Soon. Any minute." He was being carried away from friends he had stayed with in London, speeding away and not for the first time. Guys making money, living at a hundred miles an hour, brilliant, loving it, you've got to do it man, not forever but, you could get a job easy, give it a go why don't you, you've nothing to lose. Well, and maybe some of them would come back some day, bringing their booty with them, but would they see the flash? They might, but they might be driving, they probably would be driving, and so - but only if they were looking out, and depending which way they came - they would see the past. They might stop to try to touch it. If they checked the coupon they would see a draw and two defeats.

But he, on the train, saw the future. Once before, on this same journey, in this same dawn, he saw through the window a red flame leaping in a field of barley. A great red brush of foxfire dancing across the face of some farmer's faith. And now he always saw it. The free fox in the early sun, ecstatic, and himself going home again. And again and again, always going home. And not in a haze of exile, but really going home, like a nail into wood. And the train gathering pace and the guard's voice as they left Berwick behind.

And the boy seeing the flash, the blur of the sign, and letting his breath out in a rush, and his dad giving him a big smile like another boy. Like a secret shared. And nothing needing to be said.

2

Bottle

The first day I was in I panicked. It was big and empty like a tomb, and when the hatch closed out the light and Stewart put the lock on I felt like I was the victim of some nightmarish injustice. I shuffled around in the dark, feeling the rough metal walls and corners, and - remembering the rules - peered out through the portholes without getting too close to them. All I could see was a small circle of light and some greyish, cement-like surface in the unfocused distance. I heard cars arriving and departing, doors being slammed, the voices of whining children and their organising, impatient mothers struggling to keep control. I remember thinking that I hated them all, and at the same time a vague, happier memory of my own childhood tried to assert itself, and then the first bottles came.

They didn't just drop in, they flew as if shot from a catapult. People getting rid of a boxful of old bottles don't see the inside of the bank, they imagine it. They imagine a heap of glass under each hole, and so they try to help spread the load by projecting their bottles as far into the middle of the bank as they can. I don't know the physics of it but I do know that when you line up a twelve-inch bottle and wheech it through a six-inch diameter hole it fairly travels. Right across to the other wall on occasion. That's why I panicked. I was crouched in the darkness, unsure of how much room I had to manoeuvre, and suddenly glass missiles were flying into my confined surroundings, not from just one direction but from two or three at once. Because one thing you can be sure of, as soon as one person starts everybody wants a go. Wee boys come up and lend a hand. A mother who has just parked her car hears the crash of glass and remembers her own empties which have been in the boot for three days. And of course they don't know, they don't know or else they have forgotten, that you're in there. As for me, I didn't know whether to lie flat on the floor, or hard up against the wall, or crouch in the middle with my arms over my head. I began to fly around the bank as fast as the bottles. Elegant, long-necked wine bottles, fat, rich whisky bottles, blunt, businesslike gin bottles. Jars and bottles of all shapes and sizes that once contained sauces, oils, vinegars, preserves, cleaning agents, medicines and, predominantly, alcohol. And me dodging and ducking, warding them off, catching them, missing them, striking and being struck by them. Yes, it was like a nightmare but I didn't scream. I remembered the rules. Also I knew a respite must come and I think, already, I was realising that I could get the better of them, the bottles and the people who threw them, that this was to be my kingdom, that I had chosen to be king.

How long have I been here? I don't know. I don't care either. Maybe if folk out there, maybe if they knew they'd expect me to be scratching the days on the wall with a piece of chalk. Or a piece of glass. Like they do in films. Or like political heroes that get put away by dictators for years. That guy - Gramsci was it? Did he keep a diary on the wall? No, he was probably too busy filling up notebooks. Anyway, I'm no hero. No prisoner either. I'm here of my own free will.

More or less.

Unemployable. So they told me. Never gave me a bloody chance if you ask me but nobody ever does. Ask me. Or give me a chance. Unless you call this.... Well, maybe. Yes. A chance and a choice.

They tried to get me to do anything. The number of schemes I've been on - youth schemes, training schemes, scam schemes, scab schemes, you name it I've done it. Housing schemes, now there's a laugh. Call that a house! A midden with a roof more like. Mind, that's all you get these days if you're not prepared to sign up for a rent-indexed mortgage I think they call it. But if you've no job you're not allowed. So you get the midden. Brilliant.

I'm not getting into all that again. Unemployable was the way they described me. Not that I've no qualifications. I've a couple of O grades, though I never could get enthused about these three-year Higher courses. I've seen people come out at the end of those like walking robots. "Specialisation - that's the name of the game, Gilmour," I mind the teacher saying. Nothing special about what I did, judging by the reaction at the job centre: "English, Mr Gilmour? Well, all right. But Modern Studies? It's hardly vocational. I mean to say, we are fast approaching the second decade of the century. We've left all that behind, surely." I said I was fast approaching ramming his snotty accent down his throat. I think that's when they decided to send me to Public Works. I mean, I fucking *liked* English. Poetry. I'm not a hardman. I used to read the poets, I mean real poets. At least they were trying to say something - to mean something. Even the poncey ones. And politics. Society. How the bloody world works. But of course, society doesn't exist any more.

Public Works. Basically it's full of people like me who are, so to speak, unemployable. Misfits. Non-fits. Unfits. They have to put you somewhere. Even if you're not doing much. Otherwise you can't get any money. "We're not a charity, Mr Gilmour. Haven't you read the pamphlet on Ethics and

Self-help? Haven't you *heard* of the work ethic?"

Public Works does all those bits of things that aren't done by the private agencies. Which isn't a lot. I suppose you could say that just shows the success of privatisation. Waste disposal (not in the scheme I stayed on, mind; you can walk knee-deep in garbage there). Dog wardens (armed of course - and you want to see some of the nutters that apply for those jobs). Parks (pay on admission). Whatever you once took for granted, they've sold it. It's getting difficult to cross the street these days without someone trying to charge you for the privilege.

Well, like I said, no work no money. The work's meaningless but they call it a point of principle. Nobody to get something for nothing. They tried this principle on me a few times but I didn't turn up. Didn't register. Didn't sign the forms. I suppose that proved their point, that I was immoral. Or amoral is it? So they evicted me. Then when I went for my money .... I would have taken up theft as a career but they'll shoot a shoplifter as soon as look at you these days. Too risky. I just wanted some bloody peace that was all. But I couldn't get out of town. I lost my travel permit years ago.

They wouldn't give me any money. They gave me some soup. While I was drinking it the Supervisor came and sat opposite me. "You're an awkward shite, Gilmour," he said, "but I'll give you another chance. It's the only one left, so I wouldn't waste any time thinking about it. Either you take it or you starve. To be frank, you're an embarrassment and we want you out of the way."

"What is it?" I asked between slurps.

"It's the banks," he said. There was a vacancy in the banks. The bottle-banks. Two vacancies in fact. I accepted. I mean you've got to be desperate but I was. I mean what can you do? It was my choice but I don't see what other choice I could have made. Apart from Surgical Experiments but there was no way I was getting into that, whatever they paid me.

The banks are a kind of sop to the community's conscience. Community such as it is. Also a leftover from the old conservation era. A kind of habit that won't die. In fact you could say the banks are all that's left of the community. People save up for them because it makes them feel like they're putting something back; doing something for nothing. Of course what they don't know is the stuff is just dumped anyway. They think it's recycled for Christ's sake. Public Works still keep up this pretence of having two banks - one for clear glass, one for coloured. The acceptable face of apartheid. And people stick to that religiously. I mean if you put a brown bottle in the clear glass bank, that's like a major breach of decorum or something.

The banks are huge. They used to be just wee bell-shaped things but now they're like big containers - massive skips with portholes in the sides and a padlocked hatch in the top for emptying. And for entry and exit by the operative. Operative. That's what they call you. As if you're a bloody brain-surgeon.

There was me and there was another guy going into the banks. I recognised him. An old guy, a lot older than me. He used to work for the Council - that shows you how long ago - in the village where I grew up. He didn't know me but I used to see him every day. He was a young man then. His name was Joe Z.

He was the son of Polish refugees who had settled here during the Second World War, so my mother told me. His name was Zblowski but everyone knew him as Joe Z. Maybe his parents had had great hopes for Joe to rise and make his way in the world, but it didn't work out like that. The world changed. He was a silent, easy-going, humble man with no ambitions that anybody knew of. He was silent because he couldn't speak. In every other way he led a normal life, but he didn't have the power of speech. Maybe this was due to some trauma undergone in childhood, I don't know. Or maybe it was just a terrible accident. But because he couldn't speak, people assumed he was stupid. There was no evidence for this. So they would make up their own evidence: "He must be stupid," they'd think, as they swept by in their new cars. "He wouldn't be in that job if he wasn't." Joe cleaned the roads. Before the first Reorganisation, I used to see him every day wheeling his cart with its dustbins and brushes and shovels round the streets of the village, taking his time, stopping for a smoke or a piece every so often, and watching the squirrels and birds and feeding them crumbs from his piece-box. After the Reorganisation, the cleansing department bought some very fancy motorised equipment that didn't get the leaves and dog shit out of the gutters half as well as Joe, and he got transferred to other duties. He became one of a team, working on the refuse collections and so forth. This brought him into much more contact with the other workers, whereas before he had been a solitary kind of figure. He had always seemed to me to have this totally unambitious attitude to life, bothered by nobody and bothering nobody else. I envied him. I must have been the only one. Everybody else thought he was wanting, when probably the reverse was the case: he wanted for nothing.

Then after the second Reorganisation Joe disappeared. And I moved away for a while so I don't know what became of him. And I still don't. I mean, I don't know what happened in between. All I know is, when I went to the banks, Joe was there as well. There must have been nearly twenty years between us, and you'd have thought they'd have spared an old man like Joe from the banks. But they didn't. Maybe he liked poetry too.

They took us down to the Public Works yard that afternoon and showed us round. Not that there was much to show. I mean, once you've seen the inside of one skip you've seen them all. They demonstrated the opening and closing of the hatch and the bolt and padlock that kept it secure. A bald man in blue overalls called Stewart was summoned and he displayed to us a ring full of keys which he kept attached to his belt. It was his job to check on the operatives, to deliver their food and let them out one day in seven. He didn't seem to be a happy man, but then not many people in Public Works do. I've never found out if Stewart is his first name or his surname. Then they gave us the regulations.

"No smoking. No drinking - especially not dregs, there's your health to consider. Keep moving about to a minimum - just to clear the glass away from the portholes. No singing, shouting, swearing or other noise. No radios, cassettes or personal headsets. Glass to be kept to the middle of the bank, and - most important - no putting your hands out of the holes to beg, or attract attention in any way. It upsets the public. Hand display if reported will result in instant dismissal. And you know what that means. No food, no pay, no nothing."

Of the two vacant banks, one was in the centre of town, in the swimming-pool car park, and the other was in the community centre car park in my old village. They asked if we had a preference. I didn't say anything, thinking Joe might like to go back to his old haunts, as it were, but of course Joe didn't say anything either, so they just delegated us and I got the village bank. Well, I didn't care, there didn't seem to be anything to choose between them. It's true I could have chosen to walk away. Like I said, I'm here by choice. But walk away to where? To no house, no job, no money, no food? I couldn't even walk into the hills - just wouldn't get near them without a travel permit, and even if I did I'd probably end up in a military training zone and step on a mine or something. When you've got as low as the banks, there just isn't anywhere else to go. It's supposed to be character-forming. You can only go up, restore your dignity, your self-respect, that kind of crap.

You go in the banks for three-month stints. While you're in there, they give you food and water, and they let you out once a week for some fresh air. All the time - and this is the good bit - they're paying you, paying your wages into a special account that you can't touch. After three months you can either take the money and make a fresh start, or you can go for another three months and accumulate some more savings. And so on.

You'd think most folk would want to get out after the first three months. I mean, where's the future in an old skip full of broken glass? But I've heard of men who've been in the banks for years. And I know why they do it. Why I do it. I didn't know at first. But you've got a lot of time for thinking in a bottle-bank and you get your priorities sorted out pretty quick. The first thing is, you're on your own. No bastards saying, you can't do that, you've got to do this. You're in charge and there's no one to argue about it. Your own territory. You control it. Nobody else is in it. Just you. You've got all the time you want to think, to come to terms with yourself, to come to terms with the world outside, to *be* yourself. No interference. You're not tyrannised by time, by day and night, by other people's habits. You can even become oblivious to the food deliveries coming through the portholes. You ignore them and then, finding the food amongst the bottles at your own convenience, it's almost like it's grown there, it hasn't come from outside. Only when Stewart opens up the hatch to get you out for your day off - only then do you feel someone else's rules on you again. At first, you're glad to get out into the sunlight, even though it hurts your eyes so much. But then it becomes more of a nuisance than a relief. In any case it hardly ever is sunny. It's usually rain or sleet or snow. And still nowhere to go. Can't go to the community centre or the library without membership cards. Can't go anywhere. You wander around the streets getting cold and miserable. So now I stay put. "Don't bother!" I shouted at Stewart one day when I heard him rattling away at the padlock. He must get it from the others all the time. "I've got to take the lock off," he said. "It's the regulations. You're entitled to it. I've got to unlock the hatch but it's up to you whether you come out." Too fucking right. Up to me. That's the best thing about the banks. When

Stewart unlocks the hatch I wait till he's gone and then I put my bucket out and take in the empty one, but I do it with my eyes shut tight so as not to see the light. Stewart always leaves the bucket in the exact same place. He's not daft. He knows the score.

The only time you really have to get out is once a month when they come to empty the bank. But that's not too bad. They do it at night when there's nobody much about, so you're not exposed to the light at all. And the guys who drive the collection trucks are like Stewart, they leave you alone. Hardly look at you when you come out the hatch. I just go and hunker down in a corner while they get the skip up on the hoist and tip it. It takes about five minutes and then you're back in on your own again. They never empty it completely so it's just a matter of heaping together the bottles that are left.

The other good thing is the money. All the time, every day you're in there, it's building up in that account. You can calculate it, you can just about imagine it piling up there - figuratively speaking of course. And the longer you stay, the bigger the pile gets. And it's all yours. No one can touch it, not even the taxman - you're exempt from tax in the banks. That's a good feeling.

You can make a good bed out of the unbroken bottles. Heaped into one corner they're a bit like these bean-bags you used to get, they kind of shape themselves to your body. You've got to watch for the broken ones but you get wise to it. You get wise to a lot of things in the banks.

I've got all these bits of poems going round in my head. It's good to have them but it's frustrating too, not having the whole poems. Of course a book would be no use at all in here. I've got bits about women who come and go talking of Michelangelo and hollow men and the way that the world ends. There's a lot of Yeats in there, *Innisfree* and the terrible beauty one, and there's odd lines of that one by Muir about the strange horses coming after the war, and one that starts

"And she, being old, fed from a mashed plate", that's all I can mind of that one. We must have done them in school, but of course no one knows any of that stuff any more. I remember the sound of them. Poetry's about sound I think, you don't have to understand what it means.

Yesterday - or was it the day before? - Stewart unlocked the hatch. It didn't seem like a week since he'd last been, but then time doesn't interest me any more. I drew back into my corner - a slight glassy rustling noise such as an outsider might imagine was made by the bottles settling. Leave me alone, my mind said. But he didn't. He raised the hatch a wee bit, a crack of light, something he hadn't done for weeks. I heard him calling me, softly.

"Gilmour. Are you all right? Listen, it's me, Stewart. Listen to me, Gilmour. There's been a death. It's Joe Z. He went on Tuesday - some woman reported it. Gilmour, we want you to go to the funeral. There's no one else. You were from the same village, this village. You knew him. There's no one else. Somebody has to go, it's the rules. You cared about him, didn't you? It wouldn't be right, just an official like me going. He needs a friend. Not a friend even. Someone who knew him. You knew Joe, Gilmour. Please say you'll go. You could do with the fresh air. Don't worry about a suit or anything, we'll take care of that. And you'll get paid double-time. Gilmour, are you all right?"

He knew I was all right. He knew it wasn't the bottles settling. I didn't answer. I was thinking of Joe's old hand dangling out of one of the portholes, breaking the rules, not waving but drowning, disturbing the bloody public. But that was done now. No point in getting sentimental about it. I didn't want to go to Joe's or anybody's funeral. This is me here. My wee kingdom and I rule. Nobody can touch me. I'm safe here and they won't get me outside for anything. Joe's funeral for fuck's sake. Do they think I'm daft or something?

3

Dungeon

We weren't drunk. We'd had a few drinks but we certainly weren't drunk. If we had been, we might not have been bothered. We might have crashed into Harry's flat without even noticing, although with that kind of racket going on I don't think so. Harry's flat's on the third floor, but you could hear it as soon as you came in from the street. Somebody's door taking a hell of a battering. And a loud, brawling, male voice.

What the fuck - says Harry as we made our way up the stair. He didn't need to finish. It was obvious what he was on about. The hammering stopped for a moment, then started again even more fiercely. Maybe it was Harry's door.

We got to the third floor and it wasn't. I stood around while Harry found his keys. Up there the din was something else. I mean the floor was shaking. Wee bits of plaster coming off the underside of the landing above. Harry handed me the keys saying, You put the kettle on, I'll sort this lot out, and he went up the last flight.

Well, I unlocked the door, but I didn't go in. I was worried about Harry. You don't get a racket like that and not be. I waited for him at the open door. I couldn't hear his steps on the stairs, but suddenly the noise stopped.

What's that you said pal?, says this voice. Big bruising man's voice, thick with drink. And Harry must have had to repeat himself. I said what's going on?

Mind your ain fucking business, says the voice. And I'm thinking, Oh no, there's going to be trouble.

It is my business, says Harry. That's my house downstairs and it's shaking with all this. What's the problem?

Nae problem of yours pal, says the voice. Just fuck off right?

Well, my heart was in my mouth now. You just don't say things like that to Harry. I mean, he's not a fighter, he's all right Harry, but he doesn't take that kind of thing from anybody, least of all when he's standing on his own stair.

No it is my problem see, says Harry. I mean I don't know who the hell you are pal, but I don't like the noise you're making up here at half-twelve at night. You don't even bloody stay in this flat.

I couldn't take any more of this. I was sure there was going to be a fight. I took the keys out of the lock and went up the stair.

The building kind of narrows at the top, so there are only two flats on that floor, but presumably there wasn't anybody in one of them, unless they were stone deaf. Harry was standing facing the other door, and in front of him was this really odd-looking couple. I hadn't even realised there was a woman there at all, she hadn't made a sound. Not that she needed to, one look and you knew her for what she was. Heels you could murder with, black stockings and leather skirt, and a face that was hard as glass under all the make-up. She was thin and angular and you could tell she'd had a bucket to drink and yet her eyes said she hadn't lost her head with it. She was out to take the fat bastard she was with for all she could get, you just had to look at her. Which was funny because then why didn't he see that, but when you looked at him you thought well, he was the kind of fat bastard who probably thought he was doing her a favour picking her up. He deserved to get cleaned out. He had wee pinhead eyes set back in his fat head and cropped hair and a chin that was very white and didn't look like it needed shaved that often. A really big guy, in a short nylon jacket and trainers, and even though he was fat he looked strong and fit and like he didn't lose many fights. He turned his ugly head and his dangerous wee eyes on me as I came up, and gave a kind of sneer.

Here comes the Seventh Cavalry, he says. Then he says to the woman, Well, you've nae competition anyway, darlin'. I'm not sure what that was supposed to be - a compliment to her or an insult to me, or if it was meant to goad Harry into going for him or what, but it didn't have much effect. The woman just fixed me with this stare. She didn't scowl or smile. She had long red fingernails but I don't think she wanted to scratch my eyes out. She was just observing.

And Harry says, Listen, I come in at night, I find someone I've never seen before kicking my neighbour's door to fuck, what do you expect? Either you piss off or I call the polis.

I was still watching the woman and her eyes flickered for a moment when Harry mentioned the polis. She didn't want to meet them, that was for sure. But the guy, he seemed to like being threatened by Harry. It gave his brain something to do.

You call the polis pal. I'm within my rights. Murphy said I could use his flat any time I wanted, any time I was in town. Any time you want mate, he says. I've got my rights. He just never left me the keys, that's all. You get the polis, I'll tell 'em. Bill Murphy's my mate. Murphy on the fucking door right? My mate. I'll tell 'em and then when they've gone I'll batter you fucking senseless.

Just to make his point he landed a couple of hard kicks on the door, just below the handle. It shook a lot but it didn't give. Then the woman spoke. Just leave it, she says.

Pig-eyes swung round again. You're with me right? he says to her. You're with me. I'm no with you. So keep your fucking mouth shut. Then he battered the door again.

Harry looked at me and shrugged. He walked away. Come on, he says. I'm not going to waste my breath.

So we went back down to Harry's flat and Harry phoned the polis. There's a guy causing a disturbance, he says. In fact, I think you'd call it breaking and entering, although he's not in yet.

I made some coffee in the kitchen and took it out to Harry in the hall. It's stopped, he said, his head cocked to one side. We listened to the silence. Funny that, he said. It's like when your washing-machine's making crunching noises and they send a bloke round. It never does it for him.

They must have broken and entered, I said. We laughed. But we decided to wait for the polis. We heard the street door open and shut once, but when we went to look there was no one on the stair. Then a couple of minutes later the door again, and this clumping sound. Two polis climbing up towards us. Christ those uniforms make them look big. I mean, I wouldn't argue with them. One of them was a sergeant, maybe in his forties. His sidekick was about my age, or younger. He had a nervous, fresh-faced look about him that made you want to ask him if he was happy in his work, just to see him turn pink.

We went up to the fourth floor, Harry explaining what had been going on. You could see the sergeant mentally balancing Harry's story against the dead silence that now greeted us. Of course there was no one there.

A couple, you say, said the sergeant. Had a bit to drink, you say. He was looking us up and down and I had to stop myself saying, We're not that stupid. We're hardly going to clype on ourselves are we? I kept my mouth shut though, and then the younger polis came to the rescue. What was the woman like? he says.

So it transpires they saw the tart walking down the street and hailing a taxi. She must have sneaked out carrying her shoes - she could never have gone down four flights on those heels without us hearing her. She wasn't daft, that one. Didn't fancy a chat with the boys in blue at all. But she was on her own? Defin*ate*ly, says the polis. So where's the fat guy? says Harry. So where is he? says the polis. We all stood around looking at each other.

Then the sergeant says *Ay* in a long drawn-out polis kind of way, and the rest of us followed his eyes up above the door. What do you call these windows you get above doors? A fanlight, only not in the shape of a fan, just a rectangle. Well, there was one of these there, but this one was different. Instead of being fixed solid, it was hinged along the bottom so that it could be swung inwards. A metal arm prevented it from falling more than about forty-five degrees, but that could be pushed to one side if you wanted it completely open for some reason. That was why we didn't notice it at first - because the window had been swung out of sight and it wasn't till you spotted the absence of a frame that you realised you weren't looking at glass, you were looking at thin air.

Up you go son, says the sergeant to his mate. The young polis didn't look too happy at the prospect but he knew when duty called, so the sergeant gave him a leg-up and he scrambled through the gap and dropped down into the flat. We could hear him walking away from us down the hall. Then silence.

After a minute or two - no screams, no scuffling, no sound at all - the sergeant was beginning to look a wee bit anxious. He still didn't like us much, so he was trying not to show it. Harry didn't help him out by saying cheerfully, It's a bit like old Fort Zinderneuf in *Beau Geste* isn't it? Any minute now the place will go up in smoke. I don't know if the sergeant had a clue what he was talking about. At any rate, he started hammering at the door.

We needn't have worried. There was the sound of keys being tried in locks, then the door opened and the young polis was standing there looking mighty relieved not to have had his throat cut. I found these in the kitchen, he says, holding up a bunch of keys.

What's the story? says the sergeant. That window was forced all right, says the PC, indicating some splintered wood and flakes of paint on the floor. But there's nobody here. This didn't sound right at all, so the three of us pushed past him and started looking around. Not that I could see anyway, he finished defensively.

Just an ordinary flat. A bedroom, a living-room, a bathroom, a kitchen. Nothing to it. Not much furniture. In fact, just a bare minimum - what you'd expect in a place that was only used occasionally. Harry and I looked in the bedroom and saw a big double- bed that we could have done with ourselves. But by this time the sergeant was regaining his confidence. He didn't think he ought to be letting us wander around someone else's property like this, especially as it didn't look like anything was wrong - apart from the window, that is. He started to hustle us out.

Very odd, very odd, he was saying. A big man, you said. Think he could have made it through that space? Indicating the window. Then the young PC stepped into the hall from the bathroom and says, Come and look at this. Quiet now. He signalled us into the bathroom like he was directing traffic and pointed triumphantly at the edge of the bath, where there was the dirty imprint of a shoe, and then to a trap-door in the ceiling. A sharp fellow, this polis. Probably go all the way to the top if he's a mason.

Up you go son, says the sergeant again, struggling to regain his authority. This time the PC didn't hesitate. His blood was up and he could see himself getting mentioned in despatches. He was up on the bath, pushing the trap aside and springing up into the roof like a gymnast. And it wasn't dark up there like it should have been. In fact electric light flooded out of the open trap. The PC's head reappeared. You want to see this, he says. And it seemed like he was talking to all of us, to anybody, not just to his sergeant.

Here, give us a hand up, says the sergeant. But before he could move the PC was away again. And we could hear his voice, really happy now. *Hello there. So this is your wee hidey-hole. Now just take it easy all right? Or I'll put these on you. Not a patch on some of this lot, but they'll do, and what's more I'll do you for assaulting me at the same time. That's better. Here, sergeant, I've got a present for you. Coming down now. Careful. He's some size.*

The sergeant waved us away, and we retreated into the kitchen, out of sight. There was a lot of bumping and cursing, and then we heard one of them using his radio. Soon there would be reinforcements to help remove Pig-eyes. Meanwhile they had us into the hall to ask if this was the man etc. The fat face scowled at us but he didn't say anything. Then there were a couple more polis in the flat and they were taking him away. But not before the polis, each in turn, had had a look up in the loft. There was a lot of laughing and shaking of heads, and one of them told Pig-eyes he was a dirty fucking bastard. The young one was still dead pleased with himself. He came over to us, maybe thinking we were feeling left out. Which we were. He took a statement off Harry, and got our names and addresses. Then he said, by way of conversation, We get them all. Harry looked like he wanted to argue that one, but the polis wasn't crowing about his crime detection rate. Perverts, maniacs, loonies, you name it, I've seen it. He'd matured a lot in half an hour, you might say. Or become more of a man anyway. He was almost swaggering. Sadists, masochists, men dressed up as women, women dressed up in, ken, all the gear, I've seen it, the bloody lot. But I've never seen a place like that. Must have cost a fortune. Bloody odd neighbour you've got, this Murphy fellow. Still, it's not him that's been breaking the law. It's a free country, eh? Too bloody free if you ask me.

Well, what like is it? says Harry. And the polis says, Hold on. He went over to his mates. Going to let them have a look? he asked. They all gave us the eye. Ay, says the sergeant, on you go then. But we haven't got all night.

We got the nod and Harry was off like a shot. Jumped up on the bath and hauled himself through the trap in a second. Then he pulled me up.

Well, it's a bloody torture chamber isn't it. I mean a real bloody torture chamber. Black leather upholstery everywhere, except where it was red. Benches and a couple of chairs. And a long black table, with these leather straps and stuff. And studded leather collars and whips and chains for Christ's sake, and a kind of harness hanging from a hook in one of the beams, and switches and canes and masks and God knows what else. And my knees were going weak and I felt sick - the smell of it, all that polished leather, the thought of it, that fat bastard and the whore, I mean he must have known but did she? And what about this guy Murphy for fuck's sake? It was disgusting. I turned back to the trap-door but Harry caught me by the wrist and I almost screamed. He stared at me and said quietly, All right.

Close it up, the sergeant told the PC when we came down. Pig-eyes had gone with the other two. They said we could go too.

I didn't have any coffee when we got back into Harry's flat. I was dead beat and I was upset. I just wanted to sleep. Harry said he'd be through shortly. We didn't discuss any of it. He seemed distant all of a sudden. And he sat up half the night. I know he did because I woke up to go for a pee and he wasn't in bed and the light was still on in the kitchen. Even in the morning we didn't discuss it. We just got some breakfast and read the papers, just like a normal Sunday. And now Harry's cool. It's like there's something I've done but I don't know what it is. Damn it I haven't done anything.

It's that place, that dungeon at the top of the house that's done it. I can see in his eyes that it's on his mind. It was so horrible I don't want to think about it. But somehow he's gone away from me and it's to do with that. I'm thinking, up there you'd never even hear her scream, and I'm trying to block it out of my mind. But Harry, I don't know what he's thinking at all.

4

Close

Another man I know, he told me he spent his third year at university in very bizarre circumstances: as if he were living in the middle of the seventeenth century. Or the eighteenth, was it? Whichever, it was a very *weird* experience. *Weird* was the word he used. It wasn't that he travelled in time, or believed in a previous existence. Not like that woman Ada Kay, who thought - thinks - she was - is - James IV. Or had once been. Who by coincidence re-acquired the name of Stewart through marriage. She had this "back-head interference" as a child growing up in Lancashire: ghost-memories of mud, old armour, headless corpses, a royal prerogative. Once a recognition was sparked in her by a railway poster at a station - STIRLING CASTLE - but she did not understand why she recognised it. When she was an adult she began to pursue herself back through time, often against her own will. She found herself irresistibly drawn to Scotland; the sound of Gaelic on the radio was pleasingly familiar; the Middle Scots of Henryson and Dunbar she could read and recite with ease. For years she wore a "cuirass-style" corslet, sprung with steel encasing her body. She found a last dwindling supply of brown ink, which made her handwriting look for the first time as though it *belonged to her*. In the 1950s she came to live and work in Edinburgh. Nationalism was natural to her because in an earlier Scotland she had been born to be sovereign head of a sovereign nation. History after 1513 - Mary, Knox, the Jacobites and suchlike - was curiously unreal and without significance for her. She suffered annually from mental and physical decline during August and September - her "dying time"; October was her month of "regeneration". She feared Northumberland and avoided going there, and at school had been repulsed by the mere feel and shape of a small book which brought her out in goose-pimples and which later turned out to be Scott's *Marmion*. Yet it was August when chance of circumstance finally brought her to visit Flodden Field. There she found a place soaked in her own blood: the soil and her feet "knew each other". She relived, outlived death, and then, returning from the monument, she opened the wicket-gate and stepped through into the twentieth century.

Not that you have to believe that. Not that it has to be true for her to believe it. Anyway, that's a diversion. It wasn't like that for this man I know. It wasn't that he lived, had lived, in the past. It just felt like it sometimes.

He had a room in a flat off one of those narrow closes running like fishbones from the spine of the High Street down to the Cowgate. He doesn't recall how he came by it. A contact of a friend of a friend, no doubt. You reached this flat by stepping from the close into a tiny damp courtyard smelling of urine, and from this courtyard into a dark doorless entrance at the foot of a narrow turnpike stair. You went up two flats and came to three doors. The one with no name on it was his.

When he first moved in he wanted to put his name on the door in order to be sure of getting his mail. But it seemed presumptuous to do this when his landlord, the owner of the flat, did not have his own name there. He wanted to ask the landlord about it but, having got a key from him, he found that he was not often available, coming and going at irregular intervals. My friend looked for signs of names at the foot of the stair, even outside in the courtyard. There was nothing. He returned to the flat. When he opened the door, light from the hall spilled out onto the stair, and by this light he happened to notice some pencil-marks on the wall. Ordinarily the stair was so gloomy that only someone who knew these were there would be able to see them. That someone was the postman. The marks were a number of names all of which had been scored or scribbled out. The landlord's name was not among them. My friend found a pencil and added his name below the others, thus, he hoped, solving his problem.

A week later he was driven from his bed early one morning by a furious banging on the door. It was the postman, wanting to know if he knew which flat contained the person named on an envelope he was holding. "That's me," he said, after a moment's confusion. The postman gave him his letter. My friend was about to say something more when the postman pulled a stub of pencil from his pocket and bent down to the wall. He was about to write when he stopped and stared. He stared for a very long time. He too was confused. Then he stood up sharply, stuck his pencil away again, and looked suspiciously at my friend who was still standing at the door shivering in his dressing-gown. "Smart bastard, eh," said the postman. He spat and stumped down the stair.

My friend noticed a strange thing after another week or two. Although he occasionally received letters, and although there was a small pile of mail for previous occupants of the flat on a table in the hall, nothing was ever delivered for the landlord. Of course his name did not appear on the wall, but surely the postman must have had a letter for him at some time. But nothing came. Not even electric or gas bills (there was no phone) to payment of which incidentally my friend was not obliged to contribute - this being the principal reason for his taking the room, its cheapness. He could only assume that the landlord had other property, perhaps a business address, to which all such correspondence was directed. But it was a weird set-up.

One day he went through the accumulated mail on the table to see if he could redirect any of it. He wondered why it kept coming when the names outside had been scored out. He checked the wall again, and noticed that his own name had been covered over in thick black pencil, and then written in below by another hand. What was more, it had been misspelt. He put this down to the postman's perversity. Being of a rather phlegmatic nature, he was himself more amused than irritated by this behaviour.

If his landlord did have another address, it may have been in the country, perhaps in the Highlands. This idea was prompted by the next weird thing that happened. My friend, returning late one night after a drink with some other students, found the turnpike stair even murkier than usual. There was a narrow dirty window on each flight of stairs through which a little light from a lamp in the courtyard penetrated, and, approaching the first of these windows, my friend realised that it was blocked by some ghastly object somehow suspended in front of it. He gingerly approached until he realised that the object had the shape of a body of some sort. With great courage he reached out a hand to touch it, and, having done so, leapt back with a cry. He had touched cold flesh, *and it had moved!* Now he could see the thing shifting slightly, and he could hear the creaking of rope. As his eyes adjusted to the dark, he made out a kind of harness around its bulk, and ropes rising stiffly to a hook embedded in the window-frame. By this time, however, he could see with relief that the body was not human, but that of a stag, slumped like a sack, its head only a few inches from the floor. Its antlers had been sawn off but it was a stag all right.

Not without some disgust he slid past the dead beast and on to the flat. A light inside advised that his landlord was home. My friend confronted him in the kitchen, where he found him cleaning a double-barrelled shotgun, a circumstance which obviously implicated him in the matter of the hanging stag.

"Don't you think the neighbours will object to that thing out there?"

The landlord gave a short laugh. "What neighbours?"

My friend could not deny the truth of this rhetorical retort. He had yet to clap eyes on a single other inhabitant of the stair. Nevertheless he was distinctly aware that there *were* neighbours. At night he heard doors closing, footsteps, water being run, and sometimes raised voices. Once he was woken by a screaming argument in the courtyard, but that of course might have been between lovers or other passers-by.

It was the stag that gave my friend the notion that his landlord owned or at least had access to some sporting-estate in the country. In the half-light that day brought to the stair its corpse was hardly less disturbing. My friend passed it on his way to his morning tutorial. He could not understand why it was there. But the landlord had disappeared again during the night, and in any case his manner was so taciturn that it defied questioning. When my friend returned later the animal was also away. Perhaps his landlord sold his game to a butcher.

A stag never again appeared on the stair. But often my friend would encounter pheasants, grouse, rabbits, hares, once even a fox, hanging in his face as he climbed to the flat. These bunches of dead things reminded him of those still-lifes in the National Gallery by William Gouw Ferguson and Richard Waitt, and this was what first gave him the sensation that he was living in a curious replica of *Old Edinburgh*. When the sun feebly sent a few shafts through the windows, they would illuminate hanging galaxies of motes that might not have altered their composition for centuries, and suspended within these would be the clusters of birds and animals, which would, like the stag before them, arrive and be removed without warning or ceremony. Time itself seemed to hang, barely stirring, in this atmosphere. And the building of course was very old, and retained practices that really belonged to another age. For example, at least one of the unseen residents habitually threw liquid of an unsavoury nature from a window into the courtyard below. My friend heard the smack of its arrival once, seconds before he emerged from the stair. On other occasions the sensual evidence of this practice was all too powerful, especially in dry hot weather. This however did not dissuade a young couple from copulating in broad daylight in one corner of the courtyard - my friend coming upon this scene and being himself far more disconcerted by the discovery than they were. No doubt other horrid obscenities persisted behind the doors on the stair - porridge poured into drawers, box-beds shared with vermin, sheep's heads consumed, and so forth.

My friend stayed in the flat for about nine months, but he never felt as though he *belonged*. Hours spent alone there seemed afterwards, when he ventured out to the library or to a bar, to have been brief dreams. He could not explain this: he simply had the feeling of being in a different space, "in a bubble of history". That is his own phrase. He refuses to elaborate on it.

Then one day he happened to notice that his name - the postman's version - had been scored out on the wall. By chance, the landlord was in. He was sitting at the kitchen table, and, as before, was cleaning his shotgun. A box of cartridges lay near at hand. My friend began to describe the strange behaviour of the postman. Why on earth should he want to remove his name?

"Oh, that wasn't the postman," said the landlord casually.

"Then, was it you?" demanded my friend incredulously. But the landlord didn't answer him directly. He fitted the barrels back into the stock, loaded two cartridges, snapped the gun shut and aimed it at the window. "Time for a change," he remarked, and squeezed the triggers.

There was a horrendous double explosion which reduced my friend, as he put it, to a gibbering wreck. In the singing quiet that followed, he was able to observe from the state of the glass that the cartridges must have been blanks.

He moved out that very evening, thinking he knew a hint when he was given one. He left no money to cover his outstanding rent and no forwarding address. He slept on my floor for a few days until he found alternative accommodation. And that was his experience of living in the Old Town of Edinburgh. I have no reason to doubt him, although I find it hard to believe that any postman would behave like that. My friend also doubts his own memory sometimes. Years from now, he says, he expects to go in search of that close, that courtyard, that stair - and he does not think he will find them. Certainly not the stair with its *weird* atmosphere. If you ask him why not, he just shrugs, and you know for a certainty that that is the future he believes in.

My own experience of an Edinburgh close is less dramatic. There is one which runs from the cosy shop-fronts of Victoria Street down past one of the Grassmarket hostels to emerge at the Cowgatehead. Walking down it used to be like descending a tale with a moral at its end: from douce, refined enterprise to harsh, vernacular hopelessness. There is a dogleg halfway down this narrow walk, so that from the top end you cannot see the bottom, and here all manner of muggers, rapists and beggars might lie in wait. But they do not. You used to find broken bottles, crushed cans of Special Brew, cigarette-ends and the like; and once I came across an abandoned pair of trousers. These were the discarded effects of men and women discarding themselves as they slid downhill to their fates. Now, however, this close is on the itinerary of a *Ghostly Tour of Old Edinburgh*, and nightly a score of visitors are herded along it and given frights by a man paid to masquerade as the dead. The drunks and derelicts seem to have surrendered what was once their undisputed territory to the forces of progress and fantasy, and for me too the close has lost its reality. You will notice I have not named it. If you understand me you will know why, and probably which close I mean. Today, when I stepped from it out into the Cowgate - where even now an old warehouse is being converted into exclusive flats to be sold at extortionate prices, presumably to persons who are both able to afford them and who are attracted by the idea of living in the heart of history - I was aware of a curious emptiness, as though something I thought was forever mine had been taken from me in a moment. But my brain is befuddled. I have probably drunk too much of the past.

5

Rabbit

I should go to more funerals. I should think more about death. Death is, after all, the chief end of man. I am not being flippant. I am simply stating a truth which is seldom acknowledged.

I could cite Beirut or Soweto as places where death must of necessity loom larger than here, but I have no experience of these places. The news on television is strangely unreal to me; merely a substitute for experience. In any case death there is too easily confused with violence. My imagination is quickened more by studying the history of my own country - which, happily, is what I am paid to do - than by images of a distant present. This is a national prejudice, but probably one with many parallels. No doubt Lebanese academics feel the past even in the shell-shocked chaos of their principal city. No doubt they are as frustrated by their inability to escape from it as I am reassured by its presence as a refuge, a sanctuary. For me the past is alive in streets, in fields, on mountains, coming out of the very ground upon which I walk, but seldom threatening to blow me to pieces.

Death was ever present a hundred, two hundred years ago in my country. Poverty, pestilence, disease, war, cold, murder - these formed the habits of a people. Three, four hundred years ago, plagues still visited the towns with devastating frequency. If you lived to be fifty you were old, and exceptional. Nowadays everybody reaches fifty, and all are unexceptional.

There are in society those who are called achievers; and there are the rest of us. All we achieve, at the end of the long day, is death. (The achievers, by the way, are not exceptions; they only think they are.) So we should think more upon death, instead of insisting that life can be lived evading the issue, hoping, perhaps, that it may take us by surprise. For it never does. This is the truth of the matter. Death is no surprise. You do not attend a funeral, following after the coffin and the cleric, and expect *not* to peer into that narrow, deep pit. You recognise the rattle of earth on wood before it falls.

Today I walked across the links to the sea. In a hollow where a multitude of rabbits have their homes, I saw - apart from the usual brief blizzard of scurrying scuts - a rabbit crouched in the entrance to his burrow. As I approached he did not move. I came still closer. It was a shock to me to realise, as I bent before him, that he was dead. There was no sign of that terrible, man-inflicted virus, myxomatosis; no bloodshot, weeping eyes, no swollen head. This was a rabbit, looking out at the world from his door, who had died of old age. Was he taken by surprise? I do not know, but there he was.

A thing seldom seen, I suspect. Wild animals do not often die in public. They disappear. They, it seems, must think of death in their own manner, and creep into its arms in dark, intimate places with an enviable readiness. We are discreet, too, in our own socially organised way. We do not, as a rule, curl up in the street or drop dead at the shop-counter. But we hide from death, not with it.

I mention all this because yesterday I buried my father. My father is dead and I have no children. It was inevitable, in these circumstances, that I should turn my face towards death. I am not yet fifty, but it was high time that I did so.

6

True Crime

By the time you read this I will be dead. I am a systematic man and I have always planned for an eventuality such as has now occurred; for the system failing. So you will find these words on paper complete a kind of package, which I present to you, dear Inspector, as a kind of file-closer: myself (defunct, of course), this explanation, and the girl.

Yes, it is about the girl. The girl with the book. This will explain everything.

Let me make myself plain at the outset. I want you to know that this has not happened through remorse. I feel nothing, and certainly not that. It is simply better this way. For me, for you, for the rest.

To begin. I am an educated man, a man of some intelligence, but not an ambitious one. My wants have been modest and few: a quiet life, a secure income, a contented retirement. It may seem a poor kind of attitude, but my aim has always been to get from cradle to grave with the minimum of fuss, my life disrupting, and disrupted by, the lives of others as little as possible. So I had hoped to continue, but now all has changed. My guard, if not my resolve, has been slipping, and now, after all this time, I have permitted myself to make a mistake. And so things cannot go on as they always have done. That is why I have come to this. I want the minimum of fuss.

I have always thought myself a tolerant man, though I am not perhaps the easiest to get on with. I am being as objective as I can, basing my claim on the available evidence: I am unmarried, I know nobody I could call a close friend, and I have no social life to speak of. My various acquaintances in my work treat me with politeness, with good humour even, but without warmth. This is not their fault, nor is it my intention to criticise. It is I - and I admit this freely - it is I who am the cold fish. And there is good reason: it is the result of a necessary, lifelong habit of self-discipline and the regulation of passions which would have overwhelmed less rigorous men.

I have been in the book trade for nearly thirty years. As a young man I worked as a publisher's sales representative - a traveller, as the term then was - for nearly four years. Then I settled in this town, and worked for some years in the book department at Berryman's, a large independent store, now closed. But though this was useful experience, I felt that books were not accorded their proper worth in such a place where so many different products were on sale. My favourite haunt during my lunch hour was in the next street, in a small but always surprisingly well-stocked bookshop called MacRae's. It is no longer there of course: that building, indeed much of the street, was demolished fifteen years ago to make way for the new shopping centre, and what is left now forms one side of a dark, dismal and usually deserted canyon, the other side being the back of the centre's multi-storey car park. Mr MacRae died the year before this catastrophe, and the shop became very run down, his son being neither interested in nor knowledgeable about the trade. By that time I was managing the general department of J&G Hewitson, as I still do today, even until this very afternoon.

The Hewitsons were astute where MacRae was only dedicated: they realised long ago that the money in books was to be made from schools and colleges, and they set about organising themselves into the most efficient suppliers of educational books for miles around. The general books, although they are, as it were, the public face of the business, have always been of secondary financial importance in a town like this. They are what people passing in the street see in the window and at the front of the shop, but at the back it is all brown paper packages, invoices to the Council, and piles of mathematics and foreign language text books.

I cannot put a definite date on it, but it must have been within a year or two of my appointment at Hewitson's that I virtually gave up reading. Before, I had prided myself on keeping abreast of the latest developments in literature, and had found MacRae's a goldmine of new or undiscovered writing. But the art of buying (from representatives, I mean) dulls one's sensibility of books as literature, and teaches one to see them merely as saleable products (which of course they are) to be assessed more by the name of the author, the publisher, the cover illustration and the price, than by the contents. For a while I continued to read and re-read the classics, but after a while even they lost their appeal. Television, I have to admit, has proved far less demanding, and often more titillating.

I suppose I suit the business: I am efficient, I am unimpressed by representatives who try to impress, and I buy enough to keep the general stock up to date without succumbing to the fads and fashions of a few months. I have two assistants whom I have trained in the use of stock control, and who record their stock cards neatly and accurately, so that when I re-order from a catalogue it is a simple matter of transferring their information to the publisher: we have 2, we require 0; we have 1, we require 1; we have 0, we require 2. And so forth. No system could operate more simply, nor more smoothly.

I have, in my twenty-one years at Hewitson's, seen many changes in the buying and selling of books. I have seen paperbacks come to dominate the shelves, and then seen hardbacks stage some sort of a recovery. I have seen the size and cover designs of books go through various phases, and I have seen the demand for different kinds of books fluctuate and sometimes die away altogether. For example, the market for Poetry is almost non-existent, in this town at any rate. This is disappointing, though scarcely surprising. On the other hand Romance and War are devoured insatiably, the former by women and the latter by men. I deplore such clichés, but I cannot dispute them.

In the mid-1960s there used to be an entire bay full of Westerns, but nowadays we keep hardly any Westerns at all. They have disappeared from the publishers' lists just as they have gone from the television schedules. What the people who used to read J.T. Edson, Will Henry and Zane Grey read now, I have no idea: perhaps they endlessly trade in trail-weary copies at John's Book Exchange, a small side-street enterprise which deals in second-hand paperbacks as a kind of front for its real profit-maker, pornography sold in sealed cellophane at the rear of the shop. But I think I know what younger people, who might once have read Westerns, are reading: Fantasy.

Fantasy takes up more and more space every month. It used to come under the general heading of Science Fiction, but by now would quite have overwhelmed the tired old Wyndhams and Asimovs that used to be so prominent, had I not decided to give it its own separate section. Fantasy books have obscure titles, apparently the outcome of a chance encounter between a ham-fist and an oversensitive word-processor keyboard: *Doom of Ydrogsabil*; *Weirdstrom in Urgarth*; and it seems to be obligatory to write Fantasy in trilogies if not trios of trilogies. The lurid covers generally depict monsters, goblins, serpents, palaces perched impossibly on pinnacles, heroic warriors and warrior-heroines (the latter usually scantily clad in a semblance of sado-erotic leather-and-steel corsetry) - a curious mixture of Arthurian legend and futuristic myth. Martians ride on winged horses, sandalled soldiers do battle with electronic swords, dinosaurs are improbably annihilated by lasers. But, really, I am indulging my prejudices - the details are unimportant. The point is, the Fantasy novel *is* today's Western. Into a wild and untamed land the author puts two opposing forces: good and evil, right and wrong. For all their violence, these books have a very moral tone. One can tell this from the pictures on the front and the blurb on the back. It is absolutely inessential to *read* them. I myself have never read a Fantasy book.

And the people who buy Fantasy - they seem to be of a type also. Young men with bad complexions and unwashed hair; pallid, plain young women dressed in ill-fitting black clothes - either too tight or quite shapeless - these are the readers of Fantasy. I do not judge. I merely observe. But what I observe is unmistakably decadent: a semi-employed, semiliterate undergrowth invading a once immaculate but now broken-walled garden. They live in damp houses and stay out of the sunlight: this much is obvious from their appearance. They are lured to Fantasy, I presume, because of what it is; because it offers them the unattainable, a glimpse at higher things; moral choice, heroism, a future. Did I say I merely observe? No, I despise them.

Then again, to act as a substitute for whatever is most desired by but least available to the reader, has always been a property of books. The armchair traveller wanders gapemouthed through guides to Venice and Florence, marvels at wildernesses and the unspeakable habits of foreigners and savages. The homely husband destined never to achieve anything worthwhile struggles through biographies of the great and good, attempts over and over to grasp the true significance of historical events, philosophical proofs and the mathematics of the universe. His frustrated wife wastes countless hours and hopeless energy on books which encourage her to reshape her body, rejuvenate her skin, or master any number of redundant old-world crafts. Young men entirely devoid of imagination buy picture-books full of sports cars, or momentous sporting moments, which supply the images for life-wishes they can barely articulate, let alone fulfil. Or they excite themselves with military history and war fiction, while their female equivalents, as I have already mentioned, gorge themselves on Romance. All these diversions, for all these people, derive from a common cause: a salivating desire to move in a world which is not, should not, or cannot be theirs.

Crime is another interesting section of the shop. I devote a lot of shelf-space to Crime, both True Crime and Crime Fiction. Let me deal with the fiction first. Traditional Crime novels - the whodunnits made famous by Agatha Christie, Ngaio Marsh, Dorothy Sayers and so forth - are not so much written nowadays. They are old-hat, and appeal to would-be Miss Marples of both sexes who are looking for something with the intellectual demand and the emotional cosiness of a *Sunday Express* crossword puzzle. Everything must fit in the end, the last fiendish crypticism make sense, no space be left unfilled to disturb the mental relief of reaching the last page. But the Miss Marples of this town at any rate seem to be on the decline. Customers now expect more violence, more psychology, more that fails to make sense. They *want* to be disturbed.

And this is closer, is it not - though still, safely, not too close - to the reality of crime? People often derive a quiet satisfaction from the idea of a diamond theft brilliantly and cleanly executed; they recoil appalled from the disgusting mess that is the legacy of a real burglary. But there has been a shift in the reading public's judgment of how much of the mess they wish to be shown: once it may have been that they were thrilled to discover *only the next morning* that the poor darling's jewels were missing; then they were excited by emptied drawers, silk and lace strewn across the bedroom floor; now they want to smell the intruder's faeces.

Here I must mention the huge amount of American Crime that is available in this country nowadays. The flipside of the American Dream, its wicked attraction, has always been crime. Of course there is a long tradition - Raymond Chandler, Dashiell Hammett, James Cain, not forgetting all that pulp fiction now being rejacketed, reclassified and resold for a great deal more than a dime: I give as an example a scribbler of disgusting little immorality tales called Jim Thompson. Contemporary Americans like Robert Parker and Elmore Leonard exploit the sleaze and sexiness of their country's underside for all it is worth. Again, I hasten to add, all this I have gleaned from the blurbs and the covers, and a quick glance at one or two pages.

What's true of Crime in general applies equally to murder. Murder by the book - by the *old* book - was always *what had been accomplished*; the corpse discovered. It was never *doing*, the hacking, the choking, the blood, the extraordinary time it can sometimes take to kill even the feeblest of victims. The motive for murder could always be rationalised: an inheritance, revenge, a lover. Today there are writers of *why*dunnits: Ruth Rendell is perhaps the most famous, in England at least. But even her books, accomplished though they undoubtedly are, are written as "entertainments", as Graham Greene used to call his less serious novels. The build-up of psychology may be convincing, but I am afraid *I* am not convinced. I have only to turn the pages of some of the True Crime books to know that I am right.

For fictional psychology, however well researched, does not, *cannot* explain the reality of murder. A fiction is constructed by an author out of his or her own experience, and so, though it includes the experience of their projected imagination, must always remain a fiction - unless, that is, the writer is an extremely brilliant criminal with a daring penchant for taking huge public risks. The writer of True Crime obviously attempts to do something else, either to get inside the thoughts of a real murderer or to stand at his elbow and watch him - on the reader's behalf - in action: one might say, either to explain the processes of a Dennis Nilsen's mind, or to stand aghast in his kitchen, witness to his seeming indifference to the head boiling in a saucepan on the stove. The second of these is comparatively easy: you only need to touch up the facts in order to stimulate the natural horror of Mr or Miss (or nowadays, most bland of all, Ms) Average. If you can add some sub-quality black-and-white photographs then the camera has done half your work for you: the scene of the crime, the mutilated body (difficult to get hold of, these ones), the ordinary suburban street where the murderer lived. It is also essential to reinforce rather than disorientate those features of a particular crime which are already imprinted in the public mind: for example, any book on the Moors Murders would be less than complete if it did not contain those famous mad, evil-eyed mugshots of Brady and Hindley that are always recycled (I was going to say "dug up") whenever the case is given renewed publicity.

But, as to myself, I have never read a True Crime book from cover to cover. My experience of them is restricted to an occasional flicking through the pages, a distasteful glance at the illustrations, when they first arrive in the shop. The work of maniacs does not interest or amuse me, though it appears to attract a large enough readership judging by the sales. Including many of those black-clad, wan-faced addicts of Fantasy.

If you have read this far, you may be disappointed in me. Not for what I have done, but for what I have not done. It may appear that I have not told you anything. But in fact I have told you a great deal. And I have only a little more to write. I have come home "feeling unwell" (unheard of, for me to be sick, I should say) in order to put this all down. I cannot speak about it. I am a private man, an educated man. I can express myself best through the medium of pen and paper.

You know me, of course. It was you who questioned me yesterday, asking about the girl who was found on Wednesday night. You showed me her photograph and she was as I remembered her - a pretty young thing, neatly dressed, conventional and quiet-looking. So she looked in the picture, but I knew her to be not so sweet and innocent under her prim exterior. I was most helpful, you said, in confirming for you what you had already ascertained, that she had been in the shop that day. Because of the book, and the receipt in the bag. You knew because of that.

You also said she had told her friend at work that she was coming back to the shop. The book was to be a gift for her boyfriend, but she realised that afternoon that he already had it. So she was coming back to change it.

I told you that she never came back. No, that is incorrect. In fact I told you the truth: that I closed the shop at 5:30 as usual and that she had not come back by then. Sooner or later, given where she was found and when, you were bound to wonder about that. Well, perhaps if she just never made it to the shop, if the time of death were as early as it could possibly have been, I could be believed. But then, she could hardly have been where she was, if she had been walking from her work to Hewitson's. From Hewitson's to her home, or to her boyfriend's, maybe. And of course the book. I should never have left the book with her. Because sooner or later - perhaps by now - the boyfriend was going to realise: "But I *don't* have *that* book!"

Yes, she came back. At a quarter to six precisely, when I was alone in the shop, locking up and putting out the lights. There was a knock at the door. At first I did not recognise her in the shadow, and I signalled that we were closed. But the knock came again, insistent. I thought one of my assistants might have forgotten something. But it was the girl.

The blue raincoat was open and her white office blouse, fastened at the collar with a brooch, and the neat grey skirt of her suit were visible to me. Her hair was well-styled and her court shoes matched a largish shoulder-bag from which she produced the Hewitson's bag. She was a picture of normality, quite unlike the cheap sluttishness of the Fantasy clientele, or so one would have thought. But she was no different, underneath her pretended decency.

She implored me with her eyes and her smile. Tonight was a special night. She begged me to let her change the book. She knew exactly what to get instead.

She blushed when she named the title. But also she gave me a look. I felt my neck grow hot, and my heart began to pound. She disgusted me. And the thought of her presenting it to the boy. She excited me.

"Wait!" I said, taking the original book from her. I went quickly to the correct shelf, checked the prices, which happened to be the same, and swapped the books.

"Thank you so much," she said, with her smile again. I did not smile back.

"I trust that one will be suitable," I said.

"Oh," she said, laughing, "it will be, don't worry."

She turned on her high heels and went off. I already had my coat on. In a few seconds I had locked the door and was following her.

The canyon, the alley where MacRae's used to be, is dark and empty even during the day. A decent girl would be ill-advised to walk there alone at night. But she did. It is a short-cut from the centre to the north side of town. She walked quickly, but did not seem afraid.

Once I had entered the alley I called to her. "Wait!" I said.

She turned and of course she knew me at once. I was the last person she had seen. She stopped and waited for me. But even though she seemed relaxed I could not risk her taking fright. I said, "Your change!" So, you see, as soon as I had started to follow her I knew what I was going to do.

"You forgot your change!" I said, coming up to her. And then I did smile. That moment, that supreme moment, when she began to realise, thinking, beginning to say out loud, "But there is no change -" just as I struck her across the mouth and then stuffed it with my woollen scarf. And into a concrete recess with her, so dank and squalid, her surprise my accomplice, and she quite helpless although not ten minutes before she had been so free with her smile and her innuendos. Barely resisting as I bundled her limbs together, preventing her from struggling, smacking her head against the concrete once, twice, three times, she may well have been dead before I could get at her underthings but it really doesn't matter at that stage.

Very clean, no blood on me at all, only my scarf which I burned later that night, sitting at the fire with an unread Dickens in my lap and the television on as normal. Only I should have taken the book. That was very foolish, but at the time I thought it would be odd if it were not found.

No, it is not just that. It has been going on too long. This was like a last fling, a file-closer of my own. Now I am very tired. The pills probably. I am tired of all this. I cannot go hunting for strangers forever, when they are all strangers. The ones whose faces I see at the shelves, all are strangers, and I recognise them only as such. But once you start that there is no stopping. There is no distinction to be made. Choice - moral, aesthetic, social, whatever - goes out of the window. If indeed it ever existed.

Don't think that I have guilt. I am not here like a snivelling schoolboy doing his lines because of guilt. I am tired. I am tired and depressed. Why? Because. Because there is no poetry any more. It isn't just that there isn't a market for it, as I said about this town. Poetry is dead. It died, I think, with Eliot, the only modern poet whose lines I can remember. And not just poetry. The literature of a whole language has passed through my hands and my hands are dry and lifeless. I do not know whether it is me or the words. And yet I can write perfectly well. I can express myself, can I not? Can I not make myself understood?

You will know perfectly well that that is a ludicrous excuse. People do not kill for poetry. That is no explanation at all. But I challenge you to think of a better.

Well, that is all I have to say. If you don't like it that is your concern, not mine. But none of this really is your concern. I did not have to write this. I did not have to tell you these things. But somehow I have to put a stop to it. I really do not want any fuss.

7

The Scene

I'm sitting in this cafe with my third cup of coffee and I'm thinking I should go home now.

It's November, a dark day getting darker. Four o'clock. I can feel the key of the flat in my pocket, pinching the skin on my thigh. I should go home. There is nothing for me here.

The waitress who has brought me the three coffees, she doesn't mind. The place is pretty quiet and it's not as if I'm keeping other people from the table. But she doesn't mind anyway. I'm no trouble. In the summer she doesn't get quiet moments like this, not with the tourists swarming through the Old Town. I wouldn't come here for a coffee in the summer, wouldn't even consider it. You'd hardly get in the door in August. But this is November and the light is going fast. There's just me and the waitress and a couple of other folk, and we're not causing each other any trouble.

In fact I think she likes me. It's probably just the mood of the place, the time. She smiled when she brought me the coffees and I smiled back. Nothing more. She's nice enough looking but I'm not here to hassle her. I should be getting home soon anyway.

I have this newspaper folded in half in front of me but I'm not really bothering with it. There was a bomb in Belfast on the front page. Now I've got it turned to the letters page where there's an argument about Scots going on, whether it's a language or a dialect. It's been going on for days. It's almost as if the argument is taking place right here in the cafe, at a table behind me, in the corner, and I'm just picking up snatches of it, and it doesn't sound important but I'm half-taking it in anyway. It's that kind of unreal feeling, but I don't know what's causing it, if it's me or the place itself. In a way I feel fine, very relaxed. But also it's as if there's something missing.

The key in my pocket presses against my leg, reminding me to go home. My third coffee is almost done.

Outside the gloom is growing. The door of the cafe swings open and into the light steps a middle-aged woman, smartly dressed in a suit, and with high heels that click as she crosses the floor. She knows where she's going: straight to the counter, behind it, to the till. She turns a small key in the till and presses a button: the till opens with a ping, at the same time it makes some calculating noises and produces a strip of paper which the woman tears off and studies. She looks in the till-drawer, pokes around in there, then slams it shut. She goes through a doorway that leads to the kitchen just as the waitress is coming out of it. The waitress says hello but the woman doesn't answer. I get the impression, briefly, that the waitress doesn't care.

In the street the weather is dry but cold. A bit of an east wind. Not a day to be hanging around in. But then there's this: through the window I can see a young man in an overcoat and beret handing out leaflets to passers-by. He's at the edge of the pavement, almost into the gutter, handing out these leaflets. In August I wouldn't give him a second thought, he'd be one of dozens on this street thrusting leaflets at the crowds, in fact he would piss me off. In August he would be promoting a show, a revue, a play and I wouldn't go. But what is it this time? A theatre, an exhibition? Or maybe it's God. Salvation. It would need to be something pretty big to keep him out on the street with that wind blowing.

The woman steps half-through the doorway. "Katrine, I want to see you now." The waitress is about to clear a table. "Just a minute," she says. "Right now," says the woman. Katrine shrugs, puts down the dirty plates, and follows her through the door. No, she doesn't care.

Some people take leaflets with an automatic reflex, scrumpling them up and dropping them in the next litter-bin. Others let them fall immediately, to be caught and blown across the street by the wind. Nobody appears to be reading them at all.

Somewhere there is a radio playing. It sounds very far away but it can't be. As if it's slightly off-station. It's not in the cafe, but I don't see where else it can be. In my head a voice makes a joke: *Listen - they're playing our song!*

"No!" says Katrine. Her voice is raised for the first time all afternoon. She sounds angry, upset.

As well as the man handing out leaflets there is one other man out there who is not hurrying to somewhere else. He is leaning at the entrance to a close, just inside. A small point of red light glowing and fading occasionally like a weak lung shows that he is smoking. Presumably he is watching something. His face is in shadow but he must be watching, waiting for something: even out of the wind it's too cold to just stand around.

My coffee is cold. The woman comes to the phone behind the counter and stabs a number with her blood-red nail. She has a hard, set look about her. Then our eyes meet and hers are ice-cold and she turns away and speaks to the wall. I can't hear much of what she says. "Now," she says loudly. "Now!"

Katrine clears the table. She has been crying.

Something makes me look suddenly towards the close. It is very dark out there. The red glow has gone.

The man with the leaflets has no leaflets left. I see the last one flutter to the ground. He rubs his hands briskly and strides off down the street.

Katrine sniffs.

I should pay the bill and go home. There is nothing for me here. But I go on sitting.

Any minute now something is going to happen.

8

Sales Pitch

A man with an artificial foot comes to the door to sell me the Word of God. The wean rushes out into the hall as soon as she hears the bell go and by the time I've switched off the iron there he is with his bad foot in the door handing the wean a wee coloured picture of Jesus. I get that picture off her and hand it straight back and she starts screaming and I slap her. This I do not need caused by a complete stranger.

"Now see what you've done," I say.

"Do you worry about the state of the world?" he asks, with this smile on as if he hasn't heard me at all. He's tall and thin with a moustache and is wearing a soft felt hat.

"You'll worry about the state of your health if you don't get your boot off my carpet," I say, and when he moves it I shut the door in his face. But I've noticed the false foot and I suppose I feel a bit sorry, especially as it isn't just his fault the wean's greiting. So when the bell goes again I open the door.

"Can't I interest you in some of our literature?" the man

says. "That's enough, Joanne," I shout as by now she is rolling on the carpet giving it maximum volume. "No," I say to the man. When he starts to open his case I'm thinking it's time to shut the door again.

"Well, then, how about some brushes?" he says, and he whips off his hat and swings the case round to show me all these brush-heads that are in it.

I can't believe it. "Hold on a minute," I say. "You've got a nerve, mister. Just now you were a Jehovah's Witness or something, now you're selling me brushes. Do you think I was born yesterday?"

The man reaches down and hands the wean a pink lump of plastic from out of his pocket. It looks like it's supposed to be an elephant. I'm about to grab it off her again but it shuts her up so I let it be. "I hope that's clean," I say. "Anyway, you haven't answered my question."

"What question was that, madam?" he says. Before I can say anything he goes on, "If you're asking me, do I bring you the Word of God or the latest in house-cleaning equipment, the truth is, I do both. But since you're not interested in the former, allow me to show you the latter." That's the way he talks, dead fancy patter. It's better than the radio.

"I thought you Jehovahs went around in pairs," I say. I'm still not letting him in the house, even though it must have been a struggle for him getting up three flights of stairs.

"Pardon me, madam," he says. "I belong to the New Light Fellowship. It is my own church, founded by myself and organised on the principles of self-improvement and decent family values. I don't hold with some of these other sects. But it would not be a falsehood to say that I am, in fact, a pair, now would it? You see, I have my spiritual hat" - and he sticks it back on - "and I have my business head" - and he sweeps it off again.

"Very clever," I say. "Actually, I don't need any brushes either. What else have you got?"

So he begins to unpack his case, right there on the landing.

I check the wean but she's all right, she's chewing the elephant into something else. It's a bit embarrassing standing there, watching him struggle with his case on the floor, dragging that foot a bit. I'm hoping Mary next door isn't in. I don't want her coming out to see what's going on.

"Furniture polish?" he says. "Ozone-friendly?" I shake my head.

"Air-freshener, ditto?

"Instant stain-remover, shifts anything?

"Shoe-cream, waterproofs as it shines, works on any colour?

"Oven-cleaner, spray it on, wipe it off, no odour?

"Dry carpet-shampoo, sprinkle and vacuum, what could be easier?

"SilvaShine, brings out the sparkle in your service?"

Each time I shake my head. After a while he puts everything back and snaps the case shut.

"That's it," he says.

"Sorry," I say. "I don't need any of that stuff. My man would go daft."

"That's all right, madam," he says, and his hat goes on again and he touches the ends of his moustache. "Quite understand. Good day to you."

Suddenly I don't want him to go. "Maybe next week," I say. "I might take something next week."

"Only call once a month in this area," he says. "Goodbye now."

I don't know what else to say. "Cheerio," I say and close the door. It's stupid but I just don't want to go back to the ironing. I'm wishing I had bought something. I pull open the door again. He's just beginning to go down the stairs.

"Wait," I say. He turns. "Isn't there anything else?"

He looks at me and then slowly comes back to the door.

"Well," he says with a smile, "I could do your windows for you."

"Is that right?" I say.

"Inside and out, front and back, twelve pounds the lot. That's a good price," he says. "A very good price indeed."

"Oh, but you couldn't," I say. I've said it before I can stop myself. "I mean, the outside. It's so high, and the ledges are so narrow."

"I know what you're thinking," he says. "You're thinking, with my foot, it would be difficult for me out there. No, no, I'm not offended. But the world doesn't owe me a living, madam. I've had to adapt. I have clips, I have a harness. A man has to have faith, you know, a man has to show initiative. This is the enterprise culture."

"The windows could do with cleaning too," I say. "Especially on the outside. The outsides have never been done since we've been here. But I don't have twelve pounds. Maybe I could save up till you come back."

"Maybe you could," he says, "maybe you could indeed. But don't let the grass grow under your feet, that's all. You might wait for me to come back, and I might never come back. Then you've got to clean those windows yourself. You know what happened to my foot? I'll tell you. Got caught in some machinery eight years ago, in the factory I used to work in. You'll never work again, they said, your working days are over. They had me written off and put out to pasture. Now look at me. I'm a self-made man. I got on my bike, so to speak. I'll turn my hand to anything, anything at all. And this is the funny thing. That factory I worked in, you know what? They knocked it down. Paid the men off and knocked it down. What do you think of that, then? Eh? What do you think of that?"

I don't like him shouting at me. The wean's dropped the pink elephant and is greiting again. I shut the door on the man. This time I keep it shut. I go and pick Joanne up.

She knows how to work the snib, that's the trouble, and she can reach it no bother. One of these days she's going to open up and Mad Max the Child Molester's going to be standing there waiting for her. I should keep the door double-locked, I know, but you kind of forget when you stagger in with her and the buggy and three bags of messages and all. You just kick it behind you and fall into a chair.

9

Home Maintenance

Gavin stared at the face in the bathroom mirror, trying to work up the enthusiasm to shave it. It was one of those mornings when he didn't exactly have a hangover but on the other hand he knew he'd been drinking the night before: the dry mouth, the slightly thick feeling of his face and scalp, and the disinclination to shave. Still, there was no escaping it: the office required a clean-shaven Gavin, and the wife Rita would soon be hammering at the door telling him to get a move on, she had to get to her work on time even if he didn't.

The cold tap was stiff again and he had to make an effort to turn it on in order to splash some water on his face and into his mouth. The hot tap was even worse. He let out a few grunts and a curse as he strained to force it on. Finally he managed it, put in the plug, and filled the basin. The taps turned off easily enough, it was getting them on that was the bugger. He shook his head at himself.

The vaguely sore head didn't even have a good story to justify it. He hadn't been out with the boys. He'd come straight home from work and sat in front of the television. Three cans before tea, another two and several drams after. And this to show for it the next day. A less than spectacular hangover to match a far from spectacular evening. Not even cheating on the wife, who'd been in the same room the whole time, doing pretty much the same thing only with less booze. Mutually apart from each other.

He splashed more water on his face, this time hot, and lathered up the soap. At this point he usually went into a kind of dwaum, re-emerging only at that moment when he found himself stiffening the upper lip in preparation for the last few strokes of the razor. When he did this it looked as though he disapproved of something going on under his nose.

"Come *on*, Gavin!" said Rita. She was standing at the open door in her coat, neatly rolled umbrella under one arm, handbag over the other. Rita neat and polished as usual, Gavin shrugging the jacket on and the tie askew, Rita's black shoes gleaming, her legs on the high heels looking sexy even at eight o'clock in the morning, Gavin glancing at them but trying not to get caught, as if he wasn't her husband, wondering why he found her sexy at the most inappropriate moments. "Your shoelace is undone," said Rita. He bent to tie it on the landing while she locked the door of the flat. He heard her muttering, "For God's sake," but he did not rise to it. They went down the stair and out of the close, Rita's shoes clip-clopping, Gavin's slip-slopping. He shuffled down the street looking for the car. Rita's voice behind him said, "It's *here*, Gavin!" He tried to make up for everything by unlocking the passenger door first. Probably she didn't even notice.

The engine started first time. This was fortunate. Rita got very frustrated when the car wouldn't start. Gavin knew you had to be patient with machines, you had to treat a cold car calmly and gently. Rita didn't have many faults, but one of them was she knew nothing about machines and another was she didn't know how to drive. This meant they had to leave home together every morning. Gavin could get to his work by bus but to get to Rita's was more difficult, involving a change of buses. So he drove her there each morning and one of her colleagues drove her back as far as the town centre in the evening, and this way she only needed one bus to get home.

Gavin thought about these arrangements as they waited at the first set of lights. Everything fitted into place, it seemed, and yet, really, everything was contrived - the awkward shapes of different lives forced into a semblance of unity.

Behind them a horn sounded angrily. Gavin moved off with a jerk, aware of Rita's tight-set lips.

"You might try not to turn the taps off so hard," he said.

"What?" said Rita.

"The taps," he said, not sure why this had come into his mind just then. "You turn them off too hard. I could hardly get the hot tap on in the bathroom."

"*I* turn them off too hard?" said Rita. "That's good, coming from you. I thought I was going to burst a blood-vessel running my bath. You used the bath last night, so don't get on to me about it."

"I'm not getting on to you," said Gavin, consciously not raising his voice. "I'm just saying. You must have used the basin before me this morning. The taps were rigid."

"I didn't know I was so strong," said Rita with a sneer. "I mean, look at us, Gavin. Who's the muscle-man around here? And who's so good at sorting the plumbing and stuff? It's not me that's turning the taps off like that."

"I'll have a look at them tonight, then," said Gavin. But he knew there was nothing wrong with the taps. He'd checked all the washers and replaced any that were worn a few weeks ago, when he first noticed the stiffness. And it wasn't just one or two taps. It was all of them - the ones in the bathroom *and* the ones in the kitchen sink. That wasn't a plumbing problem, it was a human one. Force of habit, he thought grimly. Habit of force.

That evening, before Rita got home, he decided to check the taps again. He couldn't understand it. All the taps in the flat were rigid, even those on the basin in the bathroom, which he himself had been the last to use. Something had caused them to tighten up during the day.

By the time Rita came in he had managed to loosen them all, but he was dripping with sweat from the exertion. He had just gone to the fridge for a can of lager when he heard the front door close.

"Hello, there," he said. "Want a drink of something?"

"Jesus," she said, "let me get in the door." Then she saw him. "What have you been doing, running a marathon?"

"It's these taps," he explained. "I've been freeing them all. I don't know what's wrong with them."

"I don't want to hear about it," she said, taking off her coat and going into the bedroom. "All I get from you is taps, taps, bloody taps. Just sort the taps and then we can talk about something else."

He followed her into the bedroom. "Don't talk to me like that," he said, but keeping his voice as controlled as possible. "I'm just answering your question. There's something very odd about these taps, and like it or not it's affecting our lives. Yours as well as mine. I'll sort the taps, don't worry. Just don't bite my head off will you?"

She kicked off her shoes and unzipped her skirt. She had it round her knees and then she stopped and asked suddenly:

"What are you staring at?" She sat down on the bed, the skirt falling to her ankles.

He was watching her legs again. "Nothing," he said, looking away.

"Well, when I want you to watch me undressing, I'll tell you, all right?" He shrugged and turned to leave the room. Then she said, "Sorry, it's been a long day. I'll take that drink when you've sorted the taps."

"They're sorted," he said. But they weren't.

Rita had to ask him to help her shift the kitchen taps when she was making the tea. They were stuck fast again, even though he'd loosened them only half an hour before. This was very strange, but at least she had to accept what he had been saying. "You'd better get a plumber to look at them," she said.

While they were eating he brought the subject up again. "Maybe we've got one of those things that move things around," he said.

"What?" she said. She didn't know what he was talking about.

"They move furniture around. A ghost kind of thing. You have to get them exorcised."

"A poltergeist?" said Rita.

"Ay, that's it," said Gavin. "Only this one screws the taps up tight."

Rita smiled at him. It seemed the first time in months. "I think you're getting a bit obsessed about those taps," she said.

Later they drank half a bottle of whisky together in front of a crappy American movie on the television. Rita liked a lot of ice in her whisky and Gavin kept going through to the kitchen to get more for her from the fridge. He drank his own whisky straight. Each time he went to the fridge he felt an urge to test the taps on the sink. But he resisted it. Rita was right, he was probably getting obsessed with the whole business.

When he came back into the front room she had moved over to the floor beside his chair. He sat down and she put her head on his knee, reaching up with her long fingers to touch his face.

"You look tired," she said. "You could do with a break."

"We both could," he said. Then they both started to say

something else and both stopped together and laughed.

"Listen," she said, "let's go to bed early for a change. Why don't you fill up your glass and go and have a long soak in the bath. But let me go first." She stood up, a little unsteadily. "I'll just have a quick wash and get ready for bed - and I'll see you later." She put on a kind of sexy drawl for those last words as she flicked off the television.

"You're on," he said.

"How were the taps?" he asked, as she came out of the bathroom a few minutes later. She was wearing a long white nightdress, one she knew he liked her in.

"They seemed fine to me," she said. She was still putting on that drawl. "I think you fixed them good and proper this time." She kissed him as he went by. But Gavin suddenly felt uncertain about everything.

He took off his clothes and stood, holding his whisky, on the scales. He pinched the skin around his waist. He'd thought he was putting on some weight, but it didn't look too bad. Still, he should probably take more exercise.

He sat on the toilet while the bath was running, feeling a bit drunk. Right enough, the taps had turned on without any problem. He watched the water steaming up the room, and found his eye on the snib on the door. Funny that habit, locking the bathroom door, even though there was only him and Rita. He had always done it - or, at least, he couldn't ever remember not doing it.

He turned off the hot tap and put in some cold. The cold pressure was very strong and the water came out in a torrent. He tried to turn the tap back. It wouldn't budge.

He gripped the tap with both hands and tried to turn it off. The water rushed into the bath, filling it up and ruining the temperature. Gavin felt his composure going. "Come *on*, you bastard!" he gasped through gritted teeth. He had to pull the plug out to stop the bath from overflowing, but the bath was still filling faster than it was emptying.

"Right," he heard himself say, but he felt somehow distant from himself. "I'm going to sort this fucker out once and for all." He opened the cupboard under the basin and took out the plunger they sometimes needed to free blocked waste-pipes. It had a long wooden handle.

Rita's voice called to him from the bedroom. "Gavin, are you all right?" "I'm fine," he shouted back. "I've got the bastard now. It's going to be all right."

He grasped the plunger firmly at each end of the shaft, and laid it against one of the spokes on the capstan of the cold tap. He put one foot against the wall to give himself more purchase, and then pushed with all his strength. The tap didn't move. The water gushed into the bath unabated. By now it was beginning to wash over the edge onto the floor.

Gavin began to push against the tap with the shaft of the plunger in short, sharp thrusts. Finally he hit the spoke of the tap as hard as he could to make it turn, and each time he hit it he shouted, "Bastard, bastard, bastard!"

Rita was at the door now, he could picture her standing there in her nightdress, she was calling, "Gavin, what's going on, let me in!" He let out another roar of rage and smashed the plunger against the tap, and two of the spokes sheared off and hit the wall above the bath. The torrent poured out as before.

Gavin sat down on the edge of the bath, all his limbs shaking, the cold water splashing about his thighs and around his feet on the floor. Rita was banging on the door, but he didn't unsnib it. He didn't understand the tap, what was wrong with it, but it was beyond him now. He'd have to get dressed, turn off the mains in the close, and call an emergency plumber.

He sat naked on the edge of the bath, between the roar of the cold water and the hammering of Rita at the door, and thought how much that would cost.

10

A Cure

This man had suffered pain. Mild, at first, and intermittent, in recent months it had grown steadily worse, so that at last he was no longer able to ignore it, or pretend to himself that there was nothing seriously wrong. He went to see his doctor.

The doctor asked him a lot of questions and sent him to the infirmary for tests. Everybody was very kind, although they were so overworked and understaffed that the man was embarrassed at putting them to so much trouble. Eventually they said he could go home.

He had an appointment with his doctor the following week. The doctor was a young man. He too was kind. He told the man, who was in his late forties, that he had cancer. He didn't smoke, he drank only in moderation, and he ate a healthy diet. Nevertheless he had cancer. It was one of these things.

It was also very late in the day, so to speak. If they had known about it sooner - if he had come to them sooner....

No, the doctor didn't mean it was the man's fault, of course he didn't. But time was a factor in the treatment of the disease, and in this case, well, by now it was unfortunately a negative factor.

A bed in the infirmary would be available for him in a week's time. The treatment was difficult and long. Meanwhile he should relax as best he could at home, taking the drugs which the doctor would prescribe for him. The doctor would call on him to see how he was.

The man asked the doctor to tell him, frankly, if there was anything they could do; if there was *really* anything they could do. He had heard that this kind of cancer was virtually incurable, and he would rather know now if the treatment had little chance of success.

The doctor said he would not be doing his medical duty if he denied that there was any chance of success. But it was true, this was a particularly bad kind of cancer. And the time factor did have to be taken into account. It wasn't a good outlook.

The man thanked the doctor for his forthrightness and went home. He did not go to the chemist for the drugs. He did not go to the library to borrow books to relax with. He did not phone all his friends and relatives to explain what had happened. (He was not married.) He went home and sat, thinking about something he had always meant to do.

In a cupboard he found an old rucksack and a one-man tent. He had not used them for years, but they seemed to be in reasonable shape. He also found a sleeping-bag and opened it out to air it. He took his old walking-boots and polished and waterproofed them. Then he collected all these things, together with some old clothes, in a pile at the foot of his bed.

He was very tired by now and in some considerable pain. He could not eat, although he felt quite weak. But he was determined to do this thing. There was a place he had never been, a place he had always kept back for an emergency, as some people save money for a rainy day. Well, this was an emergency, there was no doubt about it. His main worry was that he might have left it too late.

He knew the name of the place but he would not speak it. It filled his mind, a phrase in a language of which he knew only a little, although it was all around him. He did not know why this place held such importance for him, but it had done so for a very long time. It was a mountain. He thought of it as the magic mountain, and that was what he needed and was hoping for - a wee bit of magic.

He also needed three days: a day of rain, a day of wind, a day of sun.

He slept as well as he could that night, and was up early in the morning, packing his things into the rucksack. It hurt to bend and it hurt to stand, but his mind shouted at his body and forced it to go on. When he was ready he allowed himself one small luxury: he phoned for a taxi to take him to the station.

So he went by taxi and by train and then by bus. That still left him with a good mile or two to walk before he reached the foot of the mountain. It was a dull afternoon in May, cool but not wet. This was what suited the man best. He set off along the narrow road, then along a track, and finally began to climb.

It was slow work but now that he had arrived here he was in no great hurry. In fact he had all evening, all night if he needed it. But his progress, though painful, was steady, and before the light failed completely he had reached the last of the false summits and was looking about for a relatively flat patch of ground on which to pitch his tent.

He woke early, before dawn, having slept fitfully and in great discomfort from a combination of the pain inside him and the fact that he had slipped down into one corner of the tent during the night. He was hungry but he had no food. In any case he knew if he ate he would be sick. He put on his boots and crawled out onto the mountain.

The light came up and he was alone in the world. Mountains and forests and lochs stretched away to the west and to the north, but the clouds were thickening and he could not see clearly into the distance. Mist and cloud gathered around the shoulders of the mountain. The rain came, soft and gauze-like to begin with, then heavier and heavier until it was drenching, drowning him to the bone. A day of rain. It was what was required.

He stood near to the summit of the mountain, soaking up the rain, cold at first, then his body warming his wet clothes, then cold again. He measured the wetness of the rain against the pain he was carrying, and this made the rain more than bearable - it made it a delight. He began to shuffle around the mountain, laughing and singing disjointedly, only occasionally brought to a staggering halt by a ferocious wave of nausea and pain. Then he would grip his fists into his stomach and let the rain run with his tears over his face, into his stretched mouth.

Pain.

Rain to loosen its grip, to cleanse him, to drown it.

Some time in the afternoon he became very tired. He wanted desperately to sleep. It kept raining: he would have the mountain all to himself today. He wondered if this sleep that was coming upon him was the end. He didn't know, but he could not resist it. He went back to the tent, which he had secured against the weather, and found it still pretty dry inside. He took off his clothes, dried himself a little with a towel, pulled on some dry clothes and got into his sleeping-bag. Sleep bore down upon him, forcing him to lie, to curl. He thought of the womb, and he thought of death, and himself between the two. It could not be sweeter, he thought drunkenly, and clutching his numbed stomach he sank into sleep.

It was not death. He woke when it was dark and felt the hard, kind mountain beneath him. The pain seemed less. He slept again.

On the second morning the clouds raced away to the west, to the north, scattering faster than they could gather. The peaks and lochs seemed to be flying from him. He had not died. He had taken himself away from other people, to face death alone like an animal, and death had not come. He put on his heavy wet boots and went out onto the mountain.

The pain was back. Well, he had been almost drugged with all that rain, he told himself. He was looking for magic, not miracles. Magic took a little time to work. Now, although there were still spits and flurries of rain in the sky, they were being blown away. This was good. A day of wind.

A west wind blew and up there it blew with all its strength. Not a cold wind, but fierce, to shake the grip of the pain from the walls of his body, to batter and blast it while it lay bloated and sodden from the rain. He stood into the wind and leaned against it. He shouted at it and it ripped his voice away so fast that he thought his mouth must bleed. He leapt from the mountain and the wind threw him back onto it. He danced and it swept him off his feet. He felt that he was going mad. The pain punched and tore at him from inside and the wind felled him mercilessly. He exhausted himself and, late in the afternoon, the same thing happened: he was overcome with tiredness, and crashed blindly back to his tent to sleep.

On the third morning he knew he had the bastard beaten. The pain was extreme but this was like the devils in Legion tormenting him in their last moments. There were no swine, no sheep even, on this mountain top. Nowhere to send the devils but into the mountain itself. There was himself and the mountain, and the pain, and the sun.

The pain.

A day of sun, to dry it, to bake it, to shrink it from his insides, to leave it old and wrinkled like a shrivelled prune.

He wanted to see no one. This was a famous mountain, and the sun would put people upon it. He took down his tent, packed his belongings into the rucksack, and hid them well away from the usual path that climbers would take. He knew he probably had the morning to himself. Later he would hide.

He lay in the sun, he walked in it, he ran in it. It lit up the sky and the mountains and danced on the surface of the lochs and it burned into the depths of his pain. He rolled in agony and pummelled himself but the sun would not leave him be. Finally he rolled down the slope into a hollow and slept.

There were strips of haze across the land when he awoke. The heat was by now intense. He had no watch but he guessed it was about three o' clock. He found himself lying face down in a hollow, a hundred yards from the summit. Something was happening inside him, a kind of jolting, kicking sensation. Bands of pain stretched across his stomach where he lay. He could not turn over. His face was pressed into the coarse hide of the mountain.

Then something took over in him. He saw, as though he were a bird watching from a great height, his hands scrabbling at the ground. They became claws and attacked the ground frantically, pulling and tearing at it. It was all stones here, not much vegetation and what there was of it was tough, and beneath it the thinnest of soils and the hardest of rocks, but somehow his hands scraped a small cup shape in front of his face. A small cup shape over which he lay and retched and roared in agony as the broken crust and scum of his illness was brought up through his mouth and into the cup. The mountain received his pain and took it from him.

He lay for long, long minutes, breathless, when it was all over. Sweat had fallen in curtains across his face. With his hands he drew the curtains away. Then, slowly, with great tenderness, he began to push back the soil and stones his claws had dug up. He covered over his pain and pressed the mountain back onto itself. And he kissed its magic with great humility.

He sat up and listened. He could hear voices, though still a long way off. People were coming up the mountain. He did not want to speak to them. He went to get his rucksack; to begin the descent. To avoid them if at all possible.

Well, he might perhaps pass the time of day.

Imagine. You are climbing a mountain and you meet a man coming down. "Fine day," he says. And you have no idea!

11

Survivor

The bus full of folk because of the rain. The rain outside on the windows and the windows steamed up. A wet-clothes smell, reminding him to do his laundry. Mud-spattered plastic bags at the feet of tired-looking women. And him with his hunched shoulders and hands stuffed in pockets, looking like a man without a job again, like a man coming home from the Buroo.

He would have to get off because the bus was full and he couldn't see out through the steam. It had been all right at first, but now he felt the panic rising in him and knew he had to move even though it wasn't his stop. He stood to press the bell.

There was this whining kid in front of him, refusing to sit still. Standing up in the passage between the seats, unzipping the anorak, trying to get out of it. The woman reaching for him, pulling at the zip the bairn pulling away from her, "Nooo!" She snapping his name - Alan was it? Alec? - just as he goes "I dinna want it" or was it "want tae"? He couldn't be sure because it trailed off in a whine at the end, and then she skelped him.

The skelp. *"The word's do'nt not dinny."* She spelt them like that in her head, stupid bitch, he could tell as he slid past. He made up a history of her, just for that, and the bairn screaming now because of the skelp. Where did she come from, what made her like that, assaulting a bairn for a single word? What made her despise her own tongue and force junk medicine onto the bairn's? He couldn't quite place her, so he invented her as he stood at the door fighting down the panic. His mind felt split in two that way it sometimes did. Husband a salesman maybe, or a bank clerk, went to college, and she dreaming one day, one day to be a branch manager's wife, some half-imagined, half-hated soap-sculptured gentility that would give her a role, a speaking part, a well kent face about a douce wee toun (but she wouldn't use words like *those*!), coffee mornings and sales of work and a fancy hat to church on Sundays. Her father, no doubt about him, dead now or broken anyway, a big heavy-fisted drinking man, used to put the fear of God into her so he did, and the big hard flat of his hand on the side of her head. Mother, shrivelled and abandoned, an old peenie flapping at the tail-end of a row of corporation houses at the edge of some village somewhere, nowhere. Bastard, he thought, making up lives for innocent strangers like that. Then she struck out at the bairn again to shut him up and she didn't seem that innocent. She seemed like his wife and it wasn't a made up life at all, it was a parallel life, a former life. He jumped off the bus as soon as the doors opened, just ahead of the panic.

On the street and stuck now with the whine in his ears. "I dinna want tae." It would be with him all day, that was the way it went with him. Something would stick in his ear and that would be it. Or "I dinna want it" was it? "Tae" trailing off could be "want it" unfinished. "Want it" unfinished could be "tae" trailing off. Depended how you heard it.

It didn't matter. The skelp was for "dinna" not for any other word.

Other words.

Down doun doon.

Hey hay ha'e hae.

Cow coo coup coup cowp.

You see them the way you think them. You think them the way you read them.

In at the close, the usual smells, piss, kail, damp, wet dog. The windows steamed up at every turn, the wee narrow windows looking out on dog-crapped grass and more grey concrete.

"He'll niver hae a job for lang, him. Juist hisna got it in him." The other week there he came down the stairs and his upstairs neighbour stopped what she was saying to his downstairs neighbour at her door and they watched him go by, him smiling and them smiling daft back though they all knew who they were talking about. So much for good neighbours, neighbour, he said in his head to the first man he passed on the street, and the man stared at the pavement about ten feet in front of him with that familiar downtrodden look. So much for the community spirit of the fucking tenements. Here, look, let's go for a drink, we've got things in common you and me, like no money for example, all right let's pretend to go for a drink, just sit on a park bench somewhere and raise imaginary glasses to the certain past and the uncertain future. At least let's acknowledge each other's presence for Christ's sake.

And he had "it" in him, anyway, whatever it was the woman said he hadn't. A bloody slander so it was. So all right his nerves were in shreds and he had bad dreams and lost the head sometimes and his wife had left him taking the kids to her mother and he'd been unlucky with these last three jobs the one with the gaffer who rubbed him up the wrong way then the one that was temporary then the fight he'd got into in the third one. But he still had it in him and he could prove it.

He had a video tape. He didn't have a video, that had had to go back, but he had the tape. A three-hour tape with any amount of films and sport and commercials overlaying each other but the only bit that mattered was the first five minutes. The news. He worried sometimes that it would deteriorate in the dampness, sitting around not being used, and sometimes he carried it through the house clutching it to him under his jumper to protect it, roaming the cold rooms keeping his proof warm. People would think he'd flipped if they saw him, the neighbours if they could see him, but it was like an insurance, a solid piece of evidence that nobody could dispute. He'd like to see them try the bastards.

Anyway he didn't need a video because he had it in his head, like a scene from a classic picture. He could touch the replay button without moving a muscle. Sometimes he didn't even touch. The thing just whirred into life of its own accord and turned his eyes inside out. A bit like the bairn's voice saying "I dinna want tae" only that was outside somehow and this was definitely inside.

"*'One of the survivors, Mr Kenneth Johnson, described what he saw.'*"

And him with blood on his shirt and on his trousers too and his face bruised and cut down the left side so they shot it from the left for effect, with some of the wreckage in the background. Looking pale and shocked but still somehow realising the situation, realising this was the moment you got, the brief fame, and so speaking the way you heard these people speak on the news, these people who survived disasters the way he had.

"*'I was just sitting there, there was this terrible bang, and I was pushed back in my seat, and there was luggage and that falling on me, and then the whole carriage just started to cowp and I realised we were going down the embankment. I had my back to the engine and I got kind of buried under the luggage so I wasn't getting flung about like the others. I think that's what saved me.'*

"'*You must feel very lucky.*'

"'*Ay, I feel lucky. Lucky to be alive.*'"

You think the words the way you hear them. You say them the way you think them.

Three years gone by and you'd think you could forget when everybody else had. You'd think you could wipe the tape clean but it wasn't that, it was the bit before the news, the automatic playback that nobody else saw, the bodies falling through the carriage, coming apart, the child screaming and him still sitting pressed into the seat being hit by bags and cases and people's clothes.

He gathered up his dirty laundry and stuffed it into a council bin bag. Sometimes when he picked up a shirt, even a clean one, he saw the blood again. His bit of fame.

He found enough coins to pay for the wash but not the tumble-dry. Or he could get one go in the dryer if he didn't buy powder from the crabbit old cow that ran the launderette. Sometimes there was enough powder left in the dispenser from the last person, you had to scrape it off where it was wet and lumpy but it just about did you if you were lucky. And he was. He could prove it.

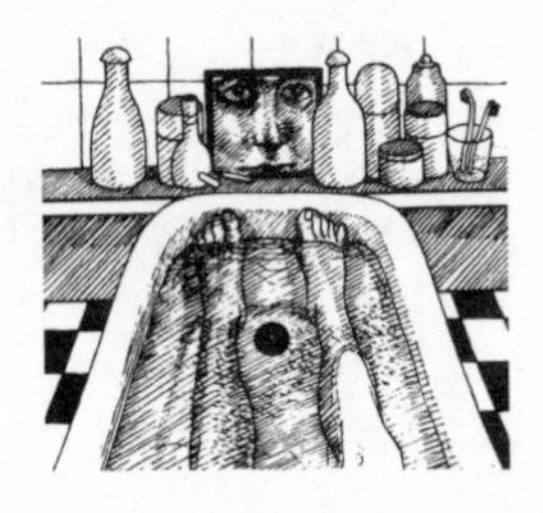

12

Bath Philosophy

He lay back in the bath and looked at himself. It was all right. He didn't take much exercise these days, but he wasn't prone to being overweight and his body, thirty-three years old, looked pretty good. If he raised himself by pushing his heels against the end of the bath his stomach muscles tightened into a hard ridge, and any sign of excess flab disappeared. The water ran off his belly, and his pubic hair, floating just below the surface, took on the appearance of a certain type of seaweed, mosslike and dark reddish in colour. And his penis became a small sea creature among the weed, washed up in the rockpool of his thighs.

His mind was always turning poetic phrases like that, and often he would produce them in the ordinary run of conversation, surprising others and even himself. But he had a flat, dry way of talking that gave a harshness to such phrases, as if he were being cynical, or stoical, in using them. Which was probably the case.

His body was quite hairy. Dark hair covered most of his chest, but stopped abruptly just below the nipples. A thin black line of it, like a seam or the place where a zip would go, ran from his breastbone straight down across his belly and navel until it was lost in the pubic seaweed. The lower parts of his arms were thick with it, so that when he raised an arm from the water the lines of hair lay plastered as evenly as a sleeve right down to the wrist. His legs were well covered too, especially below the knees; but from his chest to the tops of his thighs there was nothing at all except for that one seamlike line and then the pubic hair. His back was also completely free of hair. Some parts of his body were thick with it, others as naked as a child's. He had often looked at himself and wondered about this patchiness, what determined where the hair would or wouldn't grow. How much less hairy was he than his ancestors five hundred or five thousand years ago? Evolution was a mystery. In fact the whole business of what he and the rest of creation were doing, and why, was a mystery. Science could not solve it. It merely described it.

On the narrow shelf behind the taps was a collection of bottles and tubes and tubs: shampoo, soap, moisturiser, hand-cream, talcum powder, bath salts. His razor and shaving-foam were there. And a small mirror of Elaine's for close inspection of the facial premises. It was two-sided: one side reflected at normal size, the other enlarged the reflection, so that the user could not in fact get his or her entire face into the circle of glass. Hairs in nostrils and ears, plukes, blemishes, stray eyelashes and other flotsam and jetsam, all became massive and unavoidable on the second side of the mirror. Elaine used it for putting on her make-up, if she was wanting to make a particularly good job of it. He used it for shaving in the bath, a habit he had got into because in the winter it was more comfortable to sit in the water and shave than stand shivering in front of the mirror that hung above the basin.

Elaine had gone out to the shops. It was Saturday. The whole weekend stretched before him. He soaped and washed himself, then rinsed off and lay back in the bath.

Elaine was the most beautiful woman he knew. They had gone out together for a year, and now they had been living together for another year. They were happy. He wanted nobody else, and nor did she. Their friends thought of them as the perfect couple, just right for each other. And yet it wasn't enough. Going along like this, with this happiness, wasn't good enough. They both knew it. Their lives were useless. Neither of them *created* anything. He shuffled intangible facts and figures around computer screens all week; she edited copy for advertisements selling largely frivolous items to the insatiable consumer. At weekends they in turn consumed. Maybe this was what it was all about, but in that case why did they feel apart from their own existence, as if they were waiting for something much more significant to happen? This was what he felt. Their lives went on as if they weren't involved in them. Something needed to happen. He knew that she felt it too. But it was hard to articulate.

Sooner or later you had to find out what you were. What you were doing. The pair of you. Yourself.

What we are doing. That is all that matters.

He was having a mid-bath crisis. It wasn't unusual, but this one felt different.

What are we doing? What are we?

Something stuck in his mind. Once, years before, when he was at university, he had attended a lecture given by a famous American author. When the lecture was over someone in the audience had asked the author what inspired her to write. She had said, the human race, as a species, are storytellers. That is what we do. That is what I do.

Yes, he thought, lying in the bath, we are storytellers. Our world is constructed out of stories, millions of stories intertwined like the branches of a dense forest. We ourselves are built of stories, layer upon layer of them recording our time from womb to grave. We tell stories to remember who we are, to combat our fear of being forgotten. To tell a story is to survive.

This is also why we have children.

Years like layers, the bark on a tree or the shell that grows round a kernel until it is cast by the tree to earth. Thinking was cracking the shell, peeling off the layers.

While he thought he shaved his face, mostly by feel, sometimes using the mirror to check on his progress. The bathwater was cooler now but it was still necessary to wipe the condensation from the mirror every so often. When he had finished he rinsed the foam from his face, and sat for a minute watching the white globules speckled with little black hairs dispersing in the water. Then he lifted the razor from the side of the bath where he had laid it and began to scrape idly at a spot on his shin where the hair was thickest and darkest. Soon a small patch of nude skin emerged like an island. He stared at it as if it did not belong to him. But of course it did.

Then there was no stopping him. The hand holding the razor worked away with regular strokes, stripping off the hair like old wallpaper. It could not be stopped. He felt as if he were watching a film demonstrating some special craft which required great technical skill: fascinated, he admired the smooth stroke of the razor, the clean, fresh finish that it produced. When he had done the fronts of his legs, both below and above the knees, he stood in the lukewarm water and began to take the blade down the backs. He could not stop himself.

At last he stepped with shining legs from the hairy water. He shook his head, appalled, and then laughed out loud. How was he to explain to Elaine what had happened? Men did not normally shave their legs, and those who did had particular reasons which he did not share. He did wonder briefly what that would feel like, the nylon on his smooth legs, but it wasn't about that at all. Then, what was it about? He felt tired and confused, as if he had just woken from a dream which had disturbed him deeply but which he could not recall.

He tried to approach it philosophically. Perhaps every man should perform this exercise once in his adult life. As a kind of therapy. To remind himself of himself. To be vulnerable. To watch himself grow back.

The surface of the water was thick with hair, like the sea thick with weed after a storm. He reached in and pulled out the plug, then began to dry himself.

To be vulnerable. Was that it? He felt fresh and innocent, childlike almost. But also he felt the opposite: not innocent at all. And outside, he heard Elaine's key turning in the lock.

13

A Little Irony

Janice's first exhibition of photography caused such a furore when it opened that if Michael had not already been to bed with her he would have been too intimidated to make the attempt. In his first year at university he had taken Social Anthropology, and had been deeply affected by the belief of a certain "primitive" tribe that a woman's vagina contained sharp teeth which could, as it were, cut a man off in his prime if he in some way incurred her displeasure. As one who had also dabbled in amateur psychology and who preferred the ingenious discourses of Jung and Freud to the rigours of behaviourism, Michael never could rid his imagination of this cautionary myth when faced with the possibility of sex with a strong-minded woman. And Janice was assuredly that.

The exhibition ran for three weeks on the top floor of the city's recently refurbished municipal gallery and in that time stirred up enough political and artistic controversy to last most people a lifetime. Janice thrived on it. She was cynical enough, without abandoning belief in the integrity of her compositions, to admit that she had anticipated the fuss while putting the show together, and had known it could only do her, as artist, good. She called it "Love Hurts", and the alert critic could read that second word as either a verb or a noun, and trace its little irony throughout the photographs. Some were touching, almost sentimental portraits of lovers in the streets and parks of the city. Others, more sharply focused, were loaded with sexual references of one kind or another, straight and gay, some with fetishistic or S&M connotations - an entire commentary on the things people do and don't do to those they profess to love. It was, in the circumstances, hardly surprising that supplying such a range of images as a public service should incur the wrath of the city's *après-garde*, those noble art-going suburbanites who knew what they liked when they recognised it, except in this instance when they recognised things that they either feared or secretly rather fancied.

At the centre of the exhibition were two large pictures, which seemed to capture the mood of the whole, and which attracted much of the attention of both admirers and detractors. The first was called "The Power of Woman": shot downwards from the chest of a standing man, it showed a flaccid penis gripped by a woman's hand, the woman's arm entering the picture from behind the man; the penis rested in the woman's palm, and the nails of the fingers that curled round it were painted with a dark varnish. (All the pictures were black and white; the lighting in this one, however, cleverly accentuated the fact that the nails were painted.) The companion picture was called "The Power of Man" and its composition was almost identical, except that this time the man's own hand held his penis, the tip of which was unmistakably wet, as though it had recently ejaculated. The explicitness of this pair combined with their obvious and more subtle implications to cause a storm of debate that embraced the entire collection. Outraged Conservatives condemned the Council's subsidising of pornography and urged the police to confiscate the offending items; others protested at the apparent promotion of homosexual acts; feminists were divided as to the merits of the work, and whether Janice had exploited other women in some of the photographs; and, moving like a grey, sleazy old river, the ideologically barren public came in thousands to gaze at their deepest-held taboos and desires.

Michael certainly had ambivalent feelings towards the two central photographs, because when he looked at them he saw something of himself. This might have been because they articulated his own attitude towards the New Sexuality (as some very hip men's magazines now described it) but probably it was more to do with the fact that the penis in the pictures was his.

It was very odd to stand in a gallery and watch hundreds of people assessing the artistic qualities of your willie. The fact that his face appeared nowhere in the exhibition was a great relief, and enabled him to be reasonably relaxed as he observed crowds of complete strangers inspecting his private parts. Sometimes, it was true, he had a small urge to expose himself near the photographs and see whether anyone recognised him before he was arrested. But mostly he was quite unperturbed on his several trips to the exhibition, and wandered through it without wishing to attract attention - even to the extent of keeping his hands out of his pockets in case one of the security guards got the wrong idea about his repeated visits.

He had never before considered what female models, parts of whose anatomy appeared in "male interest" magazines, must feel like on seeing themselves in print, but he thought about it now. Whatever they were paid, he decided, it would not be worth the comfort of anonymity which he retained. And of course he was New Man enough to understand that the money was part of the exploitation: the cultural imperatives underlying their poses were quite different from whatever had made him agree to become the leitmotif of Janice's photographic statements. But he did worry about the dreamlike route by which he had reached this unusual status: what ever *had* made him agree?

They met, Janice and Michael, at a party where two of their four worlds intermingled. She was thirty-two, an artist making a modest living by doing freelance photography for magazines and newspapers, and by selling the occasional painting to a friend or relative. He was twenty-six, in the seventh successive year of his academic studies, having completed an M.A. in History and English Literature, and now writing a thesis, the working title of which was "Fiction As Life: The Intrusion of 20th Century Literature into Reality." The party was being held by Michael's tutor and his boyfriend, a sub-editor on one of the magazines Janice did work for. The two worlds not represented on this occasion were the kindly, cold bourgeois small town that was Michael's home background, and the wild, warm proletarian city scheme that had been Janice's. Michael quite enjoyed what he took to be the party's rather refined atmosphere of impending decadence, although he knew almost none of the guests. Janice, who knew many of them - and indeed some had posed, or would shortly do so, for several of the pictures in "Love Hurts" - grew bored with the lack of talent and decided not to stay long. Then she saw Michael. He seemed to be on his own, and she found him attractive. She went over to speak to him.

They had almost nothing in common but he had a beautiful smile and was willing to listen to anything she wanted to talk about. She talked too much but this didn't bother him because she wasn't pretentious and seven years of university had taught him to be amused at pretentiousness but also to avoid it in intimate relationships. And he could tell almost immediately from the interaction of their body language that their relationship was going to become intimate.

She was quite short, squat almost, but her movements were very fluid, and the bone structure of her face was very pronounced, and she had a mass of thick black hair - and all these things combined to make Michael want to touch her as soon as she approached him. Furthermore, he had reached a stage in his life when he wanted to appreciate that thrill of being seduced by an older woman which most young men feel should have been their experience as of right at the age of fifteen. After all, it happened in so many novels. This would be an important chapter in his thesis.

Janice cheated the plot by failing to initiate him into any hitherto unknown sexual experiences, and by treating him with equanimity from the outset. In the novels older women began by being in control, then gradually became obsessed with their young lovers until the latter had to be cruel to them in order to bring them to their senses. Janice seemed more to require sex than to want Michael. If he arrived at her flat on a Friday evening expecting a long weekend of libidinous pleasure he would find instead that he was directed to go for the messages, make the tea, assist with whatever creative process she was in the middle of - all these activities punctuated with couplings that seemed about as significant as the many cups of coffee they also got through. Then, if she became intent on a project, it was as if he ceased to exist for an hour or two, and he was left to wander the flat looking for things to do. Janice rented a room in it off the owner, a man who worked abroad. He kept a room for himself as a kind of home-base, but in fact he had not stayed in the place for over two years, and so she had emptied most of the furniture out of what had been his bedroom and made it into a makeshift studio, fixing heavy-duty blinds on the windows, so that she could control the natural light and supplement or replace it with her own artificial lighting as she wished. She had also converted the walk-in cupboard in the hall into a tiny darkroom. These work spaces were sparse and clean, but everywhere else Janice was outrageously untidy - dishes towered in the kitchen sink, magazines and books procreated in the living-room, and, in the bedroom, Michael was yet to positively identify the pattern of the carpet beneath the clothes that covered it. When she was busy he would find himself rather aimlessly sweeping things into piles, until Janice would suddenly notice him again and tell him to stop being so anal. But far from being bored or upset by her behaviour, he kept going back. Compared with the nebulous, unhurried atmosphere of the university, he found Janice's single-mindedness, the sense of urgency in her work, refreshing and real. He felt as if he were privileged, a witness to art in the making.

"You have a good body," she told him one evening as they lay side by side. Michael had been worrying, not too seriously, about whether she had really had an orgasm. He wondered if her comment was the nearest thing she could manage to an expression of endearment. But it wasn't.

"I mean, you have a very photogenic body. You have a smooth chest, which is useful if you want to do close-ups without having everything fur-lined, and you have good legs and arms. How would you feel about me taking pictures of you? Nude, I mean."

"It depends what you intended to do with them," he said cautiously. Caution was not the right approach with Janice.

"Don't be pathetic," she said. "It's for this show I'm working on, so of course I'd want to display them. Why not? You have a very nice body. But this is for something special. I've been thinking about it for ages."

She talked about her idea, and Michael, nervous at first, began to be interested. It was partly the significance that could be read into the pictures - he really did want to demonstrate the progressiveness of his own sexual politics - but it was also the thought of being the object of Janice's attention with her camera, in a way that he would never be without it. But then there was the problem of The Other

Woman.

Janice wasn't possessive about him; it wasn't that at all. She just couldn't think of any female acquaintances who would be willing to play the part. They were either too precious or wouldn't take it seriously.

"It has to be someone down to earth," she said. "Someone who doesn't give a toss and probably doesn't even want to know what it's all about." That was all she needed to do: say it out loud. "My sister," she said triumphantly. "She'll do it. She's perfect."

"That's the trouble with getting into this arty environment," she said later, after she had phoned her sister and arranged for her to come round the next afternoon. "You end up surrounded by middle-class wankers who make everything so complicated they can't see the wood for the trees. Now, my sister, she's dead straightforward. She can't even see the trees for the trees."

The doorbell rang and Janice went to answer it. She came back into the room with a woman of about the same height and build as her, but with short blonde hair the very opposite of Janice's long black mane. But the woman had the same aquiline nose and high cheekbones. Michael wanted to touch her too.

"This is my sister Val," said Janice. "This is Michael," she added, rather apologetically, Michael thought.

Val said hello and shrugged off her leather jacket. She held up her fingers, tipped with crimson, saying to Janice, "I forgot which hand you said, so I did both. Would have looked daft with just the one anyway."

"Fine," said Janice. "Do you want a coffee or something?"

"Ay, I'll take a cup of tea, ta, so long as it's not that Lord Grey muck you're into."

"No, I keep some chimpanzee in just for you," said Janice, as she went through to the kitchen. "What are you taking in it these days?"

"Same as ever," said Val. "Milk, two sugars and a chocolate biscuit. I'm terrible for spoiling myself," she said to Michael, thrusting a packet of cigarettes at him. He shook his head and she lit one up for herself. As she tilted her head he saw the dark roots of her hair under the bleach. Not a New Woman, he thought.

"Are you the other half of this set-up?" she asked him.

"So it would seem."

"Ay, well, my sister's going to be a big shot one day, so we better not fuck it up. Just as well our father's dead," she added. "He'd run daft if he thought she and I were getting into nudey pictures with strange men. Not that you're strange, but you know what I mean."

"What about your mother?"

"Aw, she doesn't understand our Janice. Never has and never will. I'm the one that's lived up to her expectations - six months pregnant when I got married, two years waiting on a house, the usual stuff. She can cope with that."

Janice came back with the drinks. "I was just telling Michael here about Mum," said Val. "How she doesn't understand your work."

"Ay, well I don't understand hers," said Janice. She changed the subject. Her sister seemed to Michael out of context, sitting in the big, bright room in one of Janice's basket chairs. He found himself casting surreptitious glances at her body and her bleached hair.

"You could be getting your clothes off," Janice said to him after a few minutes. He had drunk his coffee very fast, and was beginning to feel nervous about the coming session with Val. "Right," he said, in what was meant to be a businesslike manner. He didn't want to strip in front of them. "I'll just wait through in the other room, then," he said.

Fortunately the flat was warm. Janice had boosted the heating, less out of consideration for Michael than because she didn't want any goose-pimples in the pictures. She positioned him in the middle of the floor and turned to Val, about whose mouth a smile was definitely playing. "I'm just looking at your face," she assured Michael.

"You'll need to take your top off," Janice told her.

"Oh, me too now, is it?" said Val. "She's got us here on false pretences, Michael."

"Come on," said Janice. "Just be serious for ten minutes, will you? I don't want your sleeve in the way." Val pulled her jumper over her head and stood in her bra opposite Michael. He smiled at her. "I'm just looking at your face," he said. "Cheeky sod," she retorted.

"Don't you start," Janice said to him. She moved Val behind him and started adjusting the lights. Val touched him in the small of the back. "Nice bum," she said. "Please," said Michael. "This is a very delicate situation."

Janice turned on him. "You're not going to find this difficult, are you?" she said, in a tone that implied she was going to find Michael difficult. He made a sort of facial shrug, to imply that there was nothing strange, sensual or in any other way disturbing about being photographed in the nude by one sister while the other wrapped her hand round his penis. He began to concentrate his mind on long miserable walks through peat bog in the middle of winter.

It got worse when Janice set up the pose, as this involved both her hands and one of Val's moving around his groin. Val was standing very close behind him and kept balancing herself by placing her other hand on his hip. Michael was determined to prove the spirit stronger than the flesh. The outdoor exercise in his head helped. Val said:

"What is this for anyway, are you illustrating a cook book?" She put on a posh, high-pitched accent. "'First, take your beef olive....'"

"You are disgusting," said Janice.

She took some twenty or thirty shots of them, varying the lighting and the angle and occasionally changing their pose slightly. Whenever she paused to adjust the lights or the camera Val's hand would give Michael a friendly wee squeeze as if to say, "Soon be over now." About the third time she did this, as yet another image of trudging through pouring rain dissolved in his head, Michael said, "I appreciate your concern, Val, but it's wrecking my composure." She laughed and Janice said, "Don't move, either of you."

Finally she had finished with the first photograph. "Now it's just you on your own," she told Michael. Val said, "Great, I need a fag. I always do after sex."

"You haven't had sex," said Janice.

"What do you know? You didn't see what we were up to you when you were fiddling about with the lights, isn't that right, Michael?"

"Right," he said.

"If you've had sex," said Janice, "how come there isn't any semen on the end of his prick? Which is," she added, "what is required."

"Do you want me to give him a hand-job?" asked Val.

"Definitely not," said Janice. "Go and have your fag. Actually, if you want to help, go into the kitchen and mix me up some flour and a wee bit of water. Just plain ordinary white flour, Val, not my wholemeal *muck*. That ought to do the trick."

Val returned a few minutes later holding a cup with a teaspoon in it. "It's hard getting the right consistency," she said, tipping the cup towards Janice, who stirred the teaspoon a little. "That'll do," she said, and with Val still holding the cup she let most of a spoonful of the mixture dribble over the end of Michael's penis. "Lift it up," she said, tracing the spoon down the underside. He no longer felt any need whatsoever for mental hillwalking.

Afterwards, back in the front room and all of them fully dressed, Janice gave Michael the first smile of the afternoon. "That wasn't so bad, was it?"

"No, I feel I can reassure my mother that it all went

okay," he said. Val lit up another cigarette. "Seems daft to me," she said. "I mean, I'm not knocking it, Jan, I really like your stuff, but I can't get into all this heavy theory about it. At the end of the day, all you're doing is satisfying people's curiosity, isn't it? People just like looking at pictures of sex. Especially other people's sex."

"But it's more subtle than that," said Michael. "I mean, you can make a cultural statement with a photograph as well as produce something that's aesthetically pleasing."

Val gave him a look, as if to say, whichever of the two of us you're trying to impress, forget it. At least she gave him the look. Janice just shrugged and said, "You're probably right, Val."

"Listen, I'll need to be getting back," said Val. "I promised Mum I'd pick the kids up before five. Here, why don't you come down for your tea next week? Say, Wednesday. You haven't seen Daniel for ages. That's my wee boy," she told Michael. "You come too."

Michael worked at home all day Wednesday, and at three o' clock Janice phoned to say she couldn't make it to Val's, she had to go to a meeting at the gallery that evening to discuss her exhibition. Would he go on his own? She'd phoned Val and explained, it would be all right.

"What's the point of me going?" he asked. "She's your sister."

"What's the point of not going? Please, Michael. She's got food in specially. And she doesn't get out that much, she likes the company."

He agreed, and she gave him the address and advised him to get a taxi. The bus took ages and could be a bit hairy depending who was on it, and anyway it dropped you several streets from Val's house.

The scheme was in a part of the city Michael had never been in. Middle-class citizens used its name as shorthand for everything that was wrong with urban society. Liberal-minded persons in particular complained that the Government did nothing for anybody these days, but if you happened to stay in a place like P—— it was ten times worse. Unemployment, drugs, Rottweilers, housebreaking, child abuse, muggings, damp and general deprivation could all be usefully accommodated in the one word: P——.

He bought a bottle of wine and a box of chocolates and hailed a taxi in the street. When he gave the name of the street the driver had to look it up in his A-to-Z. "That'll cost you," he said grimly.

Michael huddled in a corner of the cab and expected the worst. In fact the place didn't look too bad, apart from one or two buildings with most of their windows boarded up. Val's house was in a cul-de-sac of 1950s two-storey houses, four to a block. They had a look of respectability compared to the newer, graffiti-decorated towers nearby. The driver turned his vehicle in the cul-de-sac before letting his passenger out. Michael guessed that when he wanted to leave he wouldn't have much success trying to hail a taxi in the street around here.

Val came to the door with a baby in her arms and a boy of about five at her side. "In you come," she said. He negotiated the buggy in the hallway and followed her into the kitchen. "I'm just feeding these two," she said. "We'll get ours later." The boy returned to what looked like a bowlful of cereal sprinkled with apple sauce, although it turned out that the sauce was a species of baby food which had arrived there by accident as Val fed it to the younger child. "That's Daniel, and this is Josie," she explained.

"You've got your hands full here," observed Michael helpfully. "Is there anything I can do?"

"Ay, you could pour us a glass of that wine," said Val. She seemed in good humour in spite of receiving large amounts of green sauce on her sleeve. He noticed that the varnish still on her nails was chipped and cracked, and wondered if this could be said to symbolise the overpowering drudgery of her everyday existence, and, more importantly, if he could somehow work this into his thesis with a suitable parallel from fiction.

"When does your husband get in?" he asked, opening the bottle. He was suddenly aware of being a strange man in another man's house.

"Saturday week," she said, and when Michael looked quizzically at her she said: "He works on the rigs. Two weeks on, two weeks off. If he comes home at all, that is."

Later she put the kids to their beds and disappeared for a few minutes, leaving Michael in front of the TV news in the front room. When she returned she had put on a clean blouse and touched up her face. She topped up their glasses. "I got a bottle in as well," she said.

"I would have brought more," he said, "but then Janice couldn't make it."

"Janice never can," she said. "She always has a reason not to come back here. It's like when she sees me she thinks this is what she could have been. She's escaped. Good luck to her."

"It's not so bad, is it?" Michael asked. "It doesn't seem so bad."

"It's just a different way of life, I suppose is what you could say. But sometimes it seems like a pile of shite, I swear. I mean, I didn't exactly make choices to arrive here, did I? Jan, she never stops making choices."

Michael said nothing. Val said, "She'll make one about you some day, and there'll be nothing you can do about it."

"That was a weird way of us meeting, wasn't it?" he said. "That whole afternoon was a weird experience, wouldn't you say?"

"Ay," she said. "I don't know how she manages it. Talking me into doing daft things like that. Holding your prick and everything. I mean, it's all over my head, whatever it is she wants to say. Why does she not just say it?"

"Maybe she has to express herself that way," he said.

"She's not like you. You're straightforward. You seem to know what you want."

"I don't know anything," said Val. "I'm the thick one in our family. But you, you're not thick. You're at the university and everything. And you know what, I think she humiliated you."

"I agree with what she's saying, though," said Michael. "In these pictures, I mean."

"My John, he'd think you were a fucking jessie, letting her treat you like that. Mind you, he's as thick as me."

"You keep saying you're thick," he said. "Why do you do that? Just because you haven't read a lot of books or something. You shouldn't put yourself down."

"I'm not putting myself down. I don't mean thick, really. I mean different. I think different from the likes of you and Janice. I don't know what it is. But different. She crossed some line somewhere. Maybe it was at school or maybe it's just in her, inside her. But she's not like me at all."

"I wouldn't say that. I'd say you were pretty alike."

"No, she went over to your side a while ago. I don't mind. I've nothing against it, or her, or you. But you have to face facts. Janice says the world's divided between men and women but she's more like you now than like me. I think the world's divided between people with Provvy cheques and people with bank accounts."

Michael didn't have the courage to ask her what a Provvy cheque was, but she knew he didn't know anyway.

Later, she did make a kind of meal for them - soup and toasties followed by Michael's chocolates - but the writing was on the wall. They drank the wine and went to bed and thus Michael fulfilled two more fantasies, which were to have sex with someone else's wife and to have sex with a member of the proletariat. (Janice was too far from her roots to count.) They ate the rest of the chocolates in bed and he stayed the night. She told him not to take it seriously, he wasn't the first and wouldn't be the last. She just got lonely sometimes, but she couldn't go out much what with the kids, and she had to be careful about visitors because of the neighbours. She seemed very efficient about it all. Sister like sister, he thought. Maybe they'd set the whole thing up between them, and he just floated along with it.

Janice's exhibition went on to tour a succession of private galleries in England and Wales. The public galleries all took fright and made their excuses.

She and Michael stopped seeing each other shortly after the photo session.

Val's man came home from the rigs. And went away again. And came back. Life for her was on and off like that.

Michael never completed his thesis. First he lost interest, then his grant ran out.

"And not before time," said Janice when she heard. Or was it Val?

14

Problem

You know how you think it'll never happen to you? It happened to me last night.

My wife and I were sitting up, just the same as usual. It was about midnight. That's when she told me. I was trying to do the crossword, and she was doing her knitting. She laid the knitting on the sofa beside her and sat looking at me. "John," she said, "there's something I have to tell you."

I put down the paper and looked back at her. "What?" I asked. Her expression made me uneasy.

She said, "I've been meaning to talk to you about this for a long time, but it never seemed to be the right moment. Or I didn't have the courage. But I have to tell you."

Now I was expecting the worst. I couldn't think what she was going to say, but it sounded bad. I thought, to be honest, she was going to tell me she was having an affair, although I couldn't for the life of me think who it might be with. We've been a bit distant of late. I thought it must be something like that.

"Well?" I said.

"Can we have a drink?" she asked.

There was some wine in the fridge. I fetched that and got settled again.

"Well," she said, "the thing is, I've a kind of confession to make. I'm sorry, John, I don't want to hurt you, but I can't go on pretending to be something I'm not."

"What is it?" I said. "For God's sake, Pauline, tell me what's wrong!" By now I was sure it must be an affair.

She took a sip of her wine. "The fact is," she said, "I'm a man."

Like I said, you think it'll never happen to you. I just sat there. I was stunned. There's no other word for it.

She went on and I listened in a kind of daze. Yes, she said, it was hard to accept, but the facts were there. We had to be rational about it. It was like anything that revealed itself in society as unpleasant or unexpected - you always want to think it doesn't apply to you personally. People know that smoking causes cancer, or that AIDS can lie undetected for years, and yet they still continue with the fags and sleeping around without any protection. It's the same thing with sexual misplacement, my wife told me. Everybody knows the high rates of incidence these days, everybody knows that one in ten marriages ends in divorce because of it. It's just not talked about as much as the other things. (Actually, I've always thought it was one of these things that wasn't a problem *until* everyone started talking about it, but that's not a very fashionable attitude.) Everybody *knows*, said my wife, but they don't really believe. They certainly don't believe it can turn up in their own marriage.

I said it was easy to be rational at a distance. She said that was the point she was making, and that now I had to come to terms with the fact that it was happening right here in my own living-room. She quoted statistics at me in an attempt to make me understand. As many as fifteen per cent of all women are estimated to in fact be men, she said. And almost as high a percentage of men are really women. Of course these figures aren't precise, because so few people are prepared to come out with it. It's too embarrassing, or too disruptive of their lives, and so most of those affected live with their misplacement in secret. Some tell their partners, or keep it to themselves, and try to carry on as normal. Normal, I said, what's normal? Things don't seem very normal around here just now, I said.

Then I started thinking about it in more detail. The implications were almost too horrible to contemplate. "How long have you know about this?" I asked.

"About the last four years," she said. We've been married for seven. "Of course if I'd known when we were courting I'd have told you. I'd have broken off the engagement. I've always been realistic, you have to grant me that. However much I still loved you I would have known then it was never going to work."

"Do you think you've always been . . . like this?" I asked.

She shrugged. "I suppose so. I never really thought about it. Then there was all that coverage a year or two after we got married, don't you remember, about that newsreader, Angela whatshername, who came out as a man? And that MP, John Parkhouse, the one who resigned and became an actress? It all got stirred up around then. There was a lot of stuff in the Sunday papers and the women's magazines, and after a few months I began to recognise feelings and experiences that were the same as my own. I was like you, I couldn't believe it at first. I wanted to kill myself. Then I thought, no, that's no solution, you have to learn to accept it. You can't deny yourself like that."

I tried to recall what our life had been like four years ago. Certainly Pauline had gone through a period of great depression. It was about then that she had grown more discreet, had stopped walking around the bedroom naked, had taken to locking the bathroom door. And sex. About that time she'd become reserved, prudish as I thought, about sex. She would do it less and less often, and only in bed, with the lights out.

Sex. I closed my eyes, I wanted to close my mind, against the realisation that was dawning on me. How had she, how did we . . . ?

I said, "There's a lot of things I'm not clear about, but we can talk about them later. Right now I need some proof. I need you to show me."

"What, now?" she said.

"For Christ's sake, Pauline," I shouted, "it's the least you can do. If you're going to hit me with this, you have to prove it."

"All right," she said. "Keep your voice down." She stood up and unzipped her jeans, then pulled them down with her knickers. I didn't have to look very long.

"Okay," I said, as she dressed again. I felt sick. "Okay, I believe you. Christ, what are we going to do?"

She was very calm. I felt like I was climbing the wall, but I suppose she was more used to the idea. She said, "I think we should go to see Andy." Andy is our lawyer. "He'll have dealt with this before. Let's speak to him and see where we go from here."

"It might be more to the point if you went to see a doctor," I said. That was wrong of me, I see that now. But last night I was in shock. I felt bitter. I was clutching at straws. "I mean, couldn't you get an operation or something, so we could, well, carry on, you know, more or less as we are now?"

She was angry. She said, "You're not listening to me. I'm a man, I'm not a transsexual. I don't want an operation to suit you. I want to live my own life."

That was the bottom line really. Today I can see that. I didn't argue much more. She went on to tell me she still loved me, she wanted us to be friends if we could. I said, "Ay, sure, we can meet up for a few pints some time," but she didn't think that was very funny.

Later, lying in bed, all these thoughts in my head about

how you never know what life's waiting to mug you with around the next corner, I tried to show her I didn't mean her any harm, I just wanted the best for her. I found her hand with mine, and tried to pretend it didn't feel any different from the way it had always felt. I said, "Pauline, I want you to be happy. Whatever happens I want you to be happy. But you know what bothers me most of all?"

"Yes," she said, "I know."

We didn't have to speak. We both lay there, wondering how on earth we were going to tell the children.

15

Right Side of the Curtain

The licence-plates said "Montana - Big Sky Country", and as a huge pale moon rose on the horizon out of a bruised boiling sunset it was easy to see why. Here there was nothing above the rolling grass but sky, and, marching alongside the road, ancient-looking telegraph poles, the looping wires of which mesmerised your gaze through the window of the pick-up. The driver was a tall man with a turkey-neck and sparse curly hair who had to stoop over the wheel to see through the windshield. His tee-shirt and jeans were almost as filthy as your own; his hair looked as if it would peel off his head like moss off a stone. He'd stopped for you at the tiny immigration post on the Canadian border. He said:

"Where you folks headed anyways?"

"Anywhere," said Donnie. "Browning?" he added. It was a place on the map we'd targeted for that night.

"You got friends in Browning? Place to stay?"

"We're just sleeping rough."

"Then waddya going to Browning for?"

"It's on our way. It's just a place to aim for."

"You know it's an Indian town? Blackfeet Indians in Browning. Ain't no one there likes to see strange white folks hanging around at night."

"We'll sleep somewhere out of town," you said.

"I ain't going to Browning tonight, but I can take you through there tomorrow. You don't wanna go there tonight. You wanna stay at my place?" He had hardly looked at either of you. He hardly looked at the road either, it was so straight and so quiet. His vision bounced around with the motion of the truck. You glanced at Donnie.

"Ay, that'd be great, thanks," Donnie said.

"My wife'll fix us something when we get in. Ralph Wellman."A hard ragged hand came out to shake yours, take your names.

"Where you folks from?"

"Scotland."

There was silence, as Ralph digested this. A collection of drums and tools in the back of the pick-up jostled your rucksacks like unwelcome passengers. Oil was everywhere.

"You have much problem learning English when you come here?"

Donnie burst out laughing. You explained.

"Shit, you don't say." Next he'd be asking about electricity.

Ralph was the sort of midwest American you got rides from. Others scowled at your thumbs or yelled abuse at you as they went by. Ralph wasn't suspicious of you standing at the side of the road because he'd probably done the same himself until he got the truck. He had about as much in common with his compatriots on either coast as he had knowledge of Scotland. He was typical in a way, but also he was *unlike*: easy-going, reactionary, man's man democrat with a rifle slung along the back of the cab and a healthy devotion to the conspiracy theory of history. As he warmed up you began to enjoy his crazy company while at the same time you waited for the moment when you'd have to put in a word for the niggers, wetbacks and Injuns who were usually held to be dragging the nation through the gutter. It didn't come.

Ralph's place was a kind of campsite of corrugated iron and still more oil-drums, in the middle of which a small wooden house squatted, its window-frames warped and splitting, its mosquito-netting torn. The truck slotted in among the debris like a knife into its sheath. Ralph seemed to be some kind of orraman. That was his existence. He would have hundreds of dollars stuffed away in mattresses.

Maria was a tiny dark woman who spoke midwestern with a rich Mexican accent. She had taken history courses at a college nearby. She knew a lot about Europe but nothing seemed to have rubbed off on Ralph. He loved his mystery and suspense too much. It made everything very simple. Over soup and bread and cheese he filled you in on how the goddamned communists had control of the fluoridisation programme and soon they'd be able to knock out the whole country by pumping some chemical through the water supply. Right now they were biding their time, leaving the goddamned corporations to do their dirty work for them with their selfishness and greed undermining the independent man, the honest citizen, goddamnit the working man who could go fuck it for all they cared - "I'm sorry, Maria, but that's the way it is - she don't like me to use them words." He doted on her, needing her as a support for his eccentricity. You helped her to take things through to the kitchen and she told you how important he was to her. He'd helped her to get educated and now he gave her everything, his money, his thoughts, everything. It didn't make much sense, but then it did. Back in the other room you could hear Donnie being told that the welfare scroungers had a lot to answer for too, millions of dollars spent to save lazy people from work. Ralph knew it for a fact, he'd never been on welfare, never would be.

Ralph seemed to like you both. He took you out back

where he was constructing a mobile home out of all the bits and pieces that came his way. It had an ingenious ignition system that didn't need a key. It had two enormous fuel-tanks under it, but only one, he explained, was for fuel. The other was big enough for a man to climb into. When America's time was up, Maria was going to drive (he was teaching her) south to her home in Chihuahua, sneaking Ralph across the border at El Paso. There seemed to be no reason for this extravagance of planning, but you felt that you were privileged to be in on the secret.

You unrolled your sleeping-bags on the floor of a room with no furniture. Donnie said, "I hope he doesn't have a chainsaw." Mosquitos arrived in your ear through the holes in the netting.

In the morning they gave you breakfast, the pair of them like honeymooners, although he looked old enough to be her father-in-law. The rucksacks went back in the truck, with a plastic piece-box full of Maria's potato salad for the road. Maria waved as the truck slid out of its sheath and turned towards Browning. On the edge of town you passed a clump of small white crosses, maybe a dozen, at the roadside. You asked Ralph about it. He said the state marked the site of an automobile fatality (a goddamned corporation expression, Donnie said later) with a cross - a memorial and a warning. There had been a school bus pile-up there some years ago.

He drove you through Browning and dropped you a mile to the south. You remarked that there wasn't much sign of life in the town for half-past eight. Ralph laughed. "That ain't nothing to wonder at. This town has gotten the highest unsolved murder rate in the U.S." Indians got a raw deal, he went on. Didn't take to strange white folks. Better not to take a ride from an Indian hereabouts, said Ralph. He didn't have nothing against the Indians; but handouts and liquor had ruined them. Part of the conspiracy against the common man, he added, handing you your gear. He swung the old truck round and clattered back into town.

Donnie had his multi-coloured braces on over his tee-shirt, which didn't seem to endear him to the passing traffic. After an hour, a '65 Ford Falcon pulled up twenty yards beyond you, next to a single white cross on the verge. An Indian with his hair in braids got out and beckoned you. You dumped the two rucksacks in a trunk that could have held ten.

"You a blackfeet?" Donnie asked as he drove off.

"Uh-uh." He shook his head and picked at his flat nose. "Sioux. Headed for home. South Dakota, wanna go all the way?"

"Sure."

"I'm a rodeo clown," said the Sioux. "Gotta horse back home does tricks, yea? Where you guys from?"

"Scotland."

"Yea?" A pause. "How d'you get out on the right side of that Iron Curtain, huh?"

You looked at Donnie. He shrugged.

"Well," he began, "it's a long story."

16

Rain Dance

Several separate storms drift across the sky like kites, black tails trailing to earth. Although it is almost dark the evening retains a deep blue light, split every minute or two by a white flash. The storms hang in the distance. You feel like a novice, very small, static at the heart of an unfamiliar reel, ghosts and giants swirling round about. You hope you are far enough from the pylons if one of the dancers should swoop towards you. A few hundred yards away the trucks on Interstate 90 drone and roar. You are in some kind of wasteland, face to the emerging stars, long grass bending over your sleeping-bag. The ground is dry and firm, and you are hoping it will stay that way.

Strange how the days and memories merge. Yesterday you were among white crosses that mark the spots where Custer's troopers fell. Signs warned of rattlesnakes in the grass. Last night you slept in Indian hills near the great heads of white presidents. Now, on the plains again, you think of the vast table in the grain of which you lie, the sky that bends to meet its edges, the black dancers that spin above. You imagine the tiny country of your past, its squalls and glens and history, and you understand once again that you see no landscape for the first time, always it has been painted by the minds of others before it fills your own. This is the midwest, bland apparently, without the supposed romance or tragedy of somewhere like Glencoe, apparently, and yet how small that dark wet cut seems against the drift of these storms and the awfulness of history here. Still the memory of it is here too, in your mind, in this angry sky. It is borne in upon you suddenly how far from home you are, and how you are linked to it by nothing but your own imagination. Reality is the biting of mosquitos and the threat of rain.

Yesterday you hitched rides off ranchers and their wives, through Montana and Wyoming and South Dakota. You stopped at the Little Bighorn site, looked around the visitor centre with its audio-visual and restaurant and artefacts, and then you wandered out onto the battlefield. A couple of hundred soldiers' deaths are recorded there; but from earliest memory your sympathies were always with the Indians, and there are no crosses for them. As a boy you imagined, you thought you knew this land from the books you read and the films you saw: yesterday you sat in pick-ups and beat-up old Chevys, your eyes snatching at the names on bridges - Big Horn, Little Bighorn, Tongue, Big Piney, Little Piney, Crazy Woman, Powder - and with every creek and river crossed your childhood ebbed, and you felt the loss not just of yourself but of the other people who had once been there, been here. Then today a social worker from the Pine Ridge Reservation took you on a few miles. He didn't want to talk about his job. Yes, he admitted grudgingly, Wounded Knee was on the reservation. Sure, there had been that trouble a few years back, but - "Things have gotten quieter again, now that the media's gone." But your mind flew back much further, and from your books in Scotland you recalled a photo, ninety years old, of the slaughtered chief Big Foot, his sick, muffled body frozen in the snow as if still struggling to rise.

After the ranchers a family in a station wagon towing a big trailer picked you up and took you all the way to the Black Hills. They'd come from Yellowstone and their next appointment, on behalf of their two young sons, was with the Flintstones, a theme park near the town of Custer. The Websters were from Minneapolis, stout, white, unflinchingly suburban, all four of them. They seemed almost as surprised that they'd stopped for a hitchhiker as you were. Sun and dirt had done their work on you, so that when you stood with your thumb out at the side of the road you must have appeared almost wraithlike, a thin burnt scrap in the breeze. No sooner had they pulled over than they began to regret it. For thirty miles the parents talked to you of nothing else but the dangers of picking up hitchers, while the Websters junior glowered at you with suspicion. When a couple of hours had passed and you still had not axed them to death, the parents left you alone with their offspring at a service station while they went to buy ice-cream. The boys stuck their tongues out at you, and then showered you with spittle. The Black Hills were still sixty miles away. You would like to say you were too proud to wipe your face, but no, you lost your temper and cuffed the little bastards, knowing they would not tell.

At Custer that evening the Websters booked the trailer into a park that was recommended in the AAA guide, then, since they were going there anyway, offered to run you up to Mount Rushmore. Somewhere nearby there was an even bigger figure being carved out of another mountain: Crazy Horse riding out of the rock year by year, a century too late. The Websters weren't too bothered about that. It was incomplete. They took you to see the presidents instead. At the car park you got out your rucksack, thanked them, and slipped away. Relief shone on their faces. You could imagine her turning to him: "Never, *never* do that again."

There was a filmshow and "The Star-Spangled Banner" played. After the spotlights went out on the chiselled, blasted features of the fathers of the nation, the nation streamed back down the road to its motels and campsites. You, alone it seemed, in the Black Hills. The Sioux call this island in the plains *Paha Sapa*, sacred, a place of fonts and spires and shaded aisles. When Custer took an expedition there, two years before his death, he discovered gold as well, and the cathedral was desecrated.

You left the road and struck off into the trees. You slept on a bed of pine needles as soft as any mattress. In the early light you woke to the sound of voices. Camping in the area was strictly prohibited. You wriggled on your belly out of the bag, to the edge of the trees under which you had been lying. Twenty yards below you on the road was a jeep. Three soldiers stood beside it. They seemed to be discussing something they had found at the side of the road. Some sign of you? You watched, unmoving. Then one of them picked up some discarded rubbish from the ditch - plastic wrappers and coke cans - and you realised they weren't soldiers at all but park rangers. "Fuckin' ignorant," one of them said, as they climbed back into the jeep with their trophies. You rolled back to bed for half an hour, laughing. If you were trespassing at all, it wasn't against the rangers.

Lots of short rides today. Another rancher. A guy who gave you a couple of joints to keep you happy in case you had a long wait. A small-time businessman wanting an audience for his stories of big-time deals and sales. A born-again who took you on two miles then pulled over and asked you if you were ready to meet your Maker. As it turned out, this was not a threat, just misplaced concern. You said you were. Then a cop who drove you ten miles from the freeway just to get you off his patch. A drunk man and his dog who took you back again. Thus you were blown and buffeted like a tumbleweed towards Sioux Falls, this city, this wasteland, and these first hard splats of rain as the dancers gather overhead and the sky, like a great grey swollen sheet, begins to rip.

17

That Time We Were With The Cubans

That was the time we went up to Princeton for the weekend. It wasn't the kind of place I'd expected to find Cubans, but Jeff knew them, he knew they were there. He'd arranged with them to put us up. Jeff was from Miami Florida, in fact so were the Cubans as I found out, that's how they were acquainted. What did we go up there for, I don't remember now, a football game or something. Anyway, Princeton was something else after Philadelphia, all lawns and students in long scarfs on bikes, *very* Ivy League. We went to the football or whatever but it was really cold and the teams weren't that great anyhow, so we left and went looking for Jeff's Cuban buddies. I said, Jeff, what are these guys doing at Princeton University, I mean is Castro funding them or what? Jeff laughed, he said, Man, Castro don't give these guys shit. They're from *Miami*, man. They're loaded. I kind of hadn't thought about it but probably this meant their fathers had donated big bucks for all that covert/overt CIA shit that went on in the sixties. I mean, said Jeff, we are talking rich, I've seen Carlos put two hundred green ones on one Jai-Alai game. Didn't I tell you about their New Year party? Jesus, that was something. They barbecued a whole pig on the beach, man, a whole fucking pig. You better believe these guys, because they're not for real. You know, they'll probably just want to get in some beers and get stoned, but we can just crash in their rooms anyway. Fine, I said, is there going to be any Cuban pussy there? Jeff gave me a look, he said, If there is, man, don't you mess with it, keep your hands to yourself. I laughed at him and he said, You listen to me, I'm serious, they take that kind of thing very personal.

Well, we got to the place and there were three of them, or maybe four, but now I can't remember even their names, except Carlos, because Jeff kept talking about him after, like he was a real buddy. I don't think so. I mean, they knew Jeff, they were okay about us being there, but they were pretty laid back about everything, you know, I got the impression we could have been anybody walking in and they'd have treated us just the same. And maybe they did have a lot of bread but they wanted ten dollars from us both for the beer and pretzels. That was okay though because they had the dope, I have to say I was impressed with the dope. They each had a supply of grass in a carrier bag, it was like they had all just gone down to Safeway and picked up their groceries, which happened to include these bags full of weed. So then we started smoking it in every conceivable kind of way, joints and bongs and pipes, you name it they had it. Carlos had this special pipe he'd made out of some clear plastic tubing, it had two metal bowls for the stuff to burn in and two intricately winding tubes leading from the bowls to the mouthpiece where they came together, and there was a hole you kept your thumb pressed over while you inhaled and you could watch the smoke billow up the tubes towards you. He showed us how to do this and Jeff did it and it was hilarious, then I did it, I pushed all the air out of myself and kept my thumb on that hole and sucked at that white smoke filling up the tubes, the longest breath I could draw, and just when I was about to release my thumb I heard Carlos say, Man he is going to *die* and that did it, I let go, and I must have taken about three joints worth into my lungs all in one go. The night seemed to go well after that but I don't remember much about it except that to the best of my knowledge no Cuban chicks showed up and even if they did I wasn't in any state to cause an international incident.

I never met those Cubans again, and pretty soon after I kind of lost touch with Jeff. He was a nice guy, I suppose, he showed me around, but we weren't that close. Later he joined the U.S. Army and I believe he was involved in the invasion of Grenada, all of which doesn't exactly surprise me given his political views, which became known to me not long after that time we went to Princeton. Probably Carlos and the others finished school and made a lot of money to add to what they already had so they could indulge their expensive habits. It was marijuana in those days but they would have got into cocaine, it was going to be that kind of decade.

Me, I came home and found myself a secure position in the dole queue. It was 1980 after all, and the Tories had been in for a year. America quickly became like a dream. But I still sometimes think of the smoke filling up the tubes of that weird pipe, and I wonder what that incredible high must have felt like when I took my thumb off the hole. It was a long time ago. And I remember thinking when I signed on, things are going to get a lot worse here before they start to get better. And I was not wrong.

18

What Do You Want, How Do You Feel?

Karen and Jimmy were going through a rough patch. That was the easiest way to explain it to friends, or to divert friends from probing. "We're going through a bit of a rough patch," one of them would say when not in the company of the other. They were a private couple, and their friends were not so close that they could start hacking their way into that rough patch out of curiosity or sympathy. Mention of the rough patch was like putting up a fence. People turned away from it, embarrassed. They apologised for intruding. "I'm sorry," they said.

Maybe Karen and Jimmy wanted different things out of life. They were both young, worked hard at their jobs, and spent their money together - on holidays, in restaurants, on their house and car - but their lives remained distinct, as though on parallel lines. So long as they happened to be running alongside each other, it made sense that they should pool their resources on a mortgage and a car, on French ski-ing trips and Greek sun, on evenings out and comfort and convenience at home. But there remained this distance between them, like the gap between a pair of rails, that could never be diminished. Usually neither of them complained about it. In fact it was quite reassuring, a sign of their mutual independence. Occasionally, however, it was as if they came across a complicated junction, involving several sets of points, and the way those two lines of theirs would wriggle and jump and snake their way through was hard on the eyes, hard on the emotions. This was the rough patch. A bit rocky, was another way of putting it. Not on the rocks, mind. Just a bit rocky.

So this time it was Karen that was frustrated. She worked in a managerial capacity in the ladies' fashions department of a very big store. It was a job with responsibility and interest, but it was boring her. The routine bored her, the fashions bored her. She got a good discount on all the clothes, which was the main perk of the job, but lately she felt she was turning into some kind of In-House Woman, a walking mannequin advertising the store wherever she went. She tried looking elsewhere for clothes, and discovered she had lost her touch. The discount had made her lazy in how she chose. In her kind of work that was fatal. So she began, not very seriously, to read through the employment pages of the papers. She really didn't know what other work she could do. She didn't fancy working in retail for the rest of her days but she didn't particularly want to retrain. Meanwhile she sought relief in other ways. She gave up buying her clothes in the store, and hunted instead in small boutiques and specialist shops. (She kept buying her underwear in the store, though, because it was good quality and, with the discount, so much cheaper, and anyway it remained, as it were, beneath the surface.) Then she tried to get Jimmy to go with her to see every new film that opened in town. She scoured the Yellow Pages in search of Chinese or Mexican or Italian restaurants they had never been to. She wanted to go dancing, ten-pin bowling, ice-skating, anything. She would have been out six nights of the week if Jimmy had gone along with it.

But Jimmy was tired. Jimmy was working long hours, both at his office and at home. He was a lawyer, and he had recently been promised a junior partnership in the firm he worked for. This was an opportunity not to be missed, but it meant putting in a lot of effort, to prove he was up to the challenge. Jimmy saw his job as more important than Karen's, in the sense that it was more of a career, it had definite stages to it. And, as well, more money along the way. Jimmy kept his head down. Karen was looking over her shoulder.

Karen knew that was what Jimmy thought. She resented it. She didn't happen to believe, in fact, that there was much of a challenge in what Jimmy did. She'd seen through the mystique of the so-called professions long ago. She was the one out in the real world, and if she was looking around it was only because you had to, you had to watch your back and keep an eye out for other chances, because nothing was certain in retail, however secure the law might be for Jimmy. The ups and downs of life, of the economy generally and of the affairs of individuals too, these affected the way the shop functioned from day to day, and you could see it, you could actually see it in the way people behaved, in the things they bought or didn't buy. But the law, the law kept plodding on. She didn't mean to be spiteful, but she could see Jimmy becoming a bit of a plodder himself, even though he was not yet thirty.

Karen went out without him, with some of the women from work, for drinks and meals and to the pictures. But she didn't like that all-girl company too much. It could get pretty repetitive. And the men were always in the background anyway - the husbands and boyfriends. She felt they should either be there in the flesh or not be there at all, but somehow they always showed up, in phone-calls home that had to be made, arrangements to meet later that had to be kept, or just in amorous tales that had to be told and told and told again. There was another departmental manager, Nancy, whom Karen preferred to go out with alone. Nancy was in charge of fabrics - curtains and covers and suchlike, and had been for years. Nancy was a lesbian, and she seemed far above all the petty chat of the other women. She and Karen got on. They understood one another. Karen enjoyed being with her and being seen with her because knowing about Nancy's lesbianism gave her an immense feeling of security and aloofness from the advances that men frequently made on them. Nancy lived with another woman, so Karen felt doubly secure. Also, she liked Jimmy to know when she was out with Nancy, because she could tell he became very jealous and excited at the thought of his wife being with such a woman. "The dyke", as he referred to her. Karen didn't get angry at him when he called her that. She knew it was a sign of his weakness.

On the other hand, there was a woman at Jimmy's work that he didn't talk much about to Karen. Her name was Jean. She was small and dark and vivacious - in many ways, in fact, she was like Karen. Maybe that was why he was attracted to her. Not that he made a pass at her or anything. He had very clear rules of his own about business and pleasure. To go out with somebody in the same place of work was, he always thought, a recipe for disaster. But even worse was to attempt to go out with somebody at work, and fail. "Never declare yourself," he said.

He said this to Jean: "Never declare yourself." They were having a drink one evening in a wine-bar, before they went home. This was not an uncommon occurrence. Jimmy, however, usually kept it vague when he got in, telling Karen that he had had a drink with "a couple of folk from work". Not that there was anything in it. Just that it was usually Jimmy and Jean on their own, and that could appear to mean what it did not. Especially as Jean was not actually seeing any man. She went out with different men now and again, she said, but none of them was steady. She had a very independent attitude. This was another thing she had in common with Karen, apart from her good looks. She seemed to know what she wanted in life. Karen, Jimmy thought, was like that. Or certainly had been. To the best of Jimmy's knowledge, though, Karen had not had any affairs since they were married five years before.

What Jimmy meant when he said to Jean, "Never declare yourself", what he was trying to do, in fact, was declare himself. To her. But so subtly that he could back out of it at any stage, and no damage would have been done, his rule-book would still be intact. So he said it as a kind of maxim, sound advice which no modern single young person in today's world should be without. Never declare yourself. Keep your own counsel. Don't make yourself vulnerable by offering yourself to someone who may reject the offer.

Jimmy was feeling vulnerable. It wasn't just because of the rough patch with Karen. It was that he felt he had let his life slip into something he hadn't intended. Not a rut, as such, because he was making progress in terms of career, experience and so on. Maybe it was his age. At twenty-eight he felt he had lost his idealism but had not yet gained the stoicism that would enable him to relax and let the world mould him. He still wanted to change the world but he knew he could not. He had lost control. Hence he felt vulnerable. Weak. In need of solace.

And Jean was warm where Karen could be so cold. Not sexually. They had a good sexual relationship, except during a rough patch. Intellectually, rather. Karen didn't open her mind to him. She didn't, well, declare herself. Sometimes he wondered why they had got married at all. But he knew why really. Five or six years ago he loved that coolness, that self-assurance. They were like two boys competing with each other in a whole range of activities - work, sports, drink, conversation - and the best thing about it was that at the end of the day or night - the day's ski-ing, say, or the night's drinking - he could take the boy to bed and find in his place this beautiful woman. But these days, what he had previously admired and grasped for, he found threatening.

Whereas Jean was warm. A real friend. He could make her laugh, really laugh, and he loved to perform for her. And she responded in kind, making him laugh as he seldom laughed at home. It was as if she brought out a side of himself that he had forgotten about. She confided in him. She told him something about her love-life, and how she preferred to control it by keeping her men at a distance. This was not to say that she didn't have a good time with them. Sometimes, she admitted, she felt like becoming a lot more involved than she was with one lover or another. A few sweet words too many, she knew, and she could find herself committed. Sometimes she liked the idea, a committed relationship, but for the most part she wanted her freedom. She was young still, only twenty-four (she had only been with the firm eighteen months), and she felt she had plenty of time.

"Never declare yourself," said Jimmy. "It's a golden rule. Even if you get on really well, I mean *really* well, with somebody, a friend, however strongly you feel for them, you can blow it in a minute by saying the wrong thing. You have to be absolutely sure you won't be knocked back before you make your move, and then, when you're sure, you move."

He stopped, realising that what he was saying had nothing to do with the sort of relationships Jean had been talking about. But she looked quizzically at him. "Then how can you ever be sure?"

And Jimmy was telling himself, as he took a drink from his bottled beer, she is looking at you neutrally, as a married man who works with her and who happens to be a friend, she is not looking at you in any other way at all. He said:

"Everything's in code. People speak in code. And if two people want the same thing, they'll start speaking in the same code. And eventually the fact that they're using the same code becomes so obvious that there's no sense in pretending any more. And that's when they both become sure."

Jean thought about this for a minute. Jimmy was thinking, she knows, does she know, she knows, does she know what I'm talking about? He almost said, "Everything I've just said was in code," but he held it back, that would have been declaring himself.

Which was what he wanted to do. If he did, and Jean responded positively, he didn't know what would happen. He couldn't imagine them having an affair. He didn't even really want such a complication in his life. It was almost as if the knowledge, the knowledge of the *potential*, would be enough to satisfy him. To know that he could have Jean, if he wanted to.

They had had several drinks. Suddenly he realised that they had been holding hands under the table, perhaps for five minutes. It wasn't really a sexual touch, more one of understanding. But their hands must have been together since before he made his little speech. So did she understand at all?

"There's only two things that matter," said Jean. "Two things you have to ask yourself. What do you want, and how do you feel? But most people daren't ask themselves those things. Because to ask what do you want means you aren't satisfied with what you've got. That's actually what it means. If people have built some kind of life for themselves, they don't want to have to admit that it's not enough. So they don't. They accept their lot. I'm not saying whether they're right or not. I'm just saying that's what they do. And how do you feel is even worse. Because if you don't feel right, then you must feel wrong - depressed, bored, angry, frustrated, something. Which means you have to take some action. That's what those two questions mean. Action. They keep you moving on. That takes a lot of energy, which most people don't have. But I think that's what it's all about, really: what do you want, how do you feel?"

"I think you may be right," sad Jimmy. But the honest truth was, he felt pretty drunk, and he hadn't taken in everything Jean had said. Some, but not all. She finished her glass and helped him to his feet.

"You're whacked," she said. "I'll share a taxi with you."

She stayed not far away from them. Karen, who had heard of Jean but knew almost nothing about her, certainly did not know this. In fact they were only ten minutes' walk apart.

The taxi dropped Jimmy off first. He was glad that the lights weren't on in the house. No questions about who else was in the taxi.

"See you on Monday," said Jean. It was the weekend, but he'd forgotten. He took out a couple of notes and once more their hands were together, for longer, it seemed to him, than was necessary for her to take the money. She kissed him swiftly. "Good night."

She kissed him. As he found his keys and heard the taxi disappear into the dark, he remembered only this. She kissed me.

When Karen arrived home an hour later she found that Jimmy had gone to bed and was sound asleep. This pleased her. She didn't want to speak to Jimmy just then. She wasn't drunk, although she'd had a few drinks. She was hungry, and made herself a cheese sandwich which she ate in front of the television, turned down low so as not to disturb him. But she wasn't really watching - some film or other that was on. She was thinking about a whole lot of things Nancy had told her.

Karen was up long before Jimmy on the Saturday. She was working, and left the house shortly after eight. Jimmy dozed discontentedly, feeling too hot and slightly hungover. Eventually, about half-nine, he fell out of bed and ran himself a bath. Later he went out for the paper and spread it on the breakfast bar while he restored himself with coffee and toast.

He knew as soon as he awoke what he was going to do. As usual he pretended otherwise, but there was no escaping it: every day she was the first thing in his mind on waking. Jean. Ten minutes' walk away.

He headed over in that direction, but by an indirect route, as if he could fool himself that he just happened to be walking past her street. He wondered what he would say. Hi. I was just passing. Thought I'd see if you were in. Scrounge a cup of coffee off you. Jean, I'm in love with you. I don't love my wife. I feel awful. I want you.

She shared a flat with another woman. He knew the number and he knew which floor. There was no one about on the street so he went into the close. Somewhere a radio was playing. He mounted the stairs, ready to scuttle down again if a door above him opened. He reached the second floor. There was her name, and another name below it, on the door. The sound of the radio was coming from her flat.

He did not knock. He stood without moving, as if for an age. He felt like a small boy, expecting reward or punishment, not knowing which. All those phrases he was going to use went round in his head. Eventually he moved away, down the stairs. The radio played on.

He trailed up the street. Behind him, on the second floor of the building, a net curtain twitched.

"It's not like that," said Nancy. "I can't explain it, but it's not about one person doing something to another, it's about two people *being* together. No competition. Complete trust. Understanding."

"But it must be a kind of test," said Karen. "A test of the relationship, seeing how far it can go."

"No," said Nancy firmly. "Not with us. It's a game. Nobody wins, nobody loses. We make it up as we go along, and there doesn't have to be any kind of set conclusion. Half the time we're pissing ourselves laughing. Remember all those games little girls play and little boys don't? That's what it's about. Believe me."

"I still think it must be a test," said Karen.

Karen and Jimmy that Saturday night. They hadn't been out. They'd watched television. Now they were lying, the two of them, in the dark, separated by a body's width of space, both of them on their backs staring at the ceiling. They did not touch, but each was very conscious of the other's presence, that they were awake and facing some kind of crisis.

"What do you want?" said Jimmy. He might have been talking to the ceiling, the way it came out.

"Mm?" To Karen, it sounded almost as if he were talking in his sleep.

"'What do you want and how do you feel?'" He lied again. "I read it somewhere. They're the only two questions worth asking."

"That's crap," said Karen. They lay there in silence for a while. Then, when he thought she must have drifted off, she said:

"I feel horny. I want to be tied up."

God knows why she let it out. It was like the first thing that came into her head. She laughed into herself.

Jimmy sat up. "Say that again?"

"I want to be tied up," she said, very matter of fact. She was daring him.

He lay down again. "Jesus," he said. "Where did that come from?"

Karen snorted. He'd have to fucking ask, wouldn't he? He'd have to analyse it.

"Who cares?" she said. "The point is, what are you going to do about it?"

"What am I going to do about it?" he echoed. Then silence.

She said, "You don't have the balls, Jimmy. Let's face it, you just don't have the balls."

She under-estimated him, as it turned out.

"I need a piss," he said, and got out of bed. When he came

back, he switched on the light and she saw, blinking, that he had the washing-line in his hand. The long line they put out in their small garden, and took in when they weren't using it because otherwise it got filthy with the rain and bird droppings and suchlike.

She giggled. "Go on, then," she said.

He was naked. He stripped the covers off her and she screamed, shielding herself, then she took off her nightdress and spread herself out like a starfish stranded on a beach and he tied her wrists and her ankles to the corners of the bed. Where the rope went from her hands to her feet it ran across her body, over one breast and her firm wee belly and cunt and down her thigh. When she moved the rope rubbed up and down that diagonal.

"Christ," she said. "I think I'm going to wet myself."

He didn't seem to hear. "Jimmy," she said. "I need to pee."

"That's tough," he said. It had been okay up until then. Nothing had happened. She had just wanted to see what *would* happen. Now she felt uneasy. She didn't really know him. Five years her husband and now, because of this, she discovers she doesn't really know him at all.

"Let me go, Jimmy," she asks quietly.

He stares at her body, appraising it. It, not her. Now she is frightened.

"I want a photograph," he says. He hurries from the bedroom in search of his camera. Karen shouts after him.

"You better untie me now, you bastard! No fucking pictures, do you hear?"

But Jimmy comes back. He has the camera, and when she raises her head she can see he is rigid with excitement. He fiddles with the camera, trying to get the flash to warm up, holding it to his ear to listen for the whine.

"No batteries," he says after a minute. She is not reassured by the fact that he takes this setback quite calmly. He is, after all, in charge of whatever happens next. "Where can I get batteries at this time of night?" It is one o'clock.

"If you don't untie me I'm going to scream blue murder till the neighbours come," says Karen.

Jimmy looks at her as if she is someone he is trying to recognise. "Shut your fucking mouth," he says. He goes over to her chest of drawers. In the top drawer she keeps her underwear, the things she still buys from her work. He takes out a pair of tights and a pair of knickers. "You'll like this," he says. "You'll shut up now."

He has to be careful stuffing the knickers in her mouth, because she snaps at his fingers like a dog. But she is helpless really, and it is easy to secure the gag with the tights tied round her head. She doesn't look like Karen any more.

"Now," he says. "A photograph." He pulls on his clothes, forcing his stiff prick into pants and trousers, grabbing a tee-shirt, not bothering with socks under his shoes. On top of the chest of drawers he finds the car-keys.

"I'll just run down to that all-night service station," he tells her. "They're bound to have batteries."

She whimpers. Her eyes are wide and full of tears.

"Shan't be long," he says. "Just relax."

She tells herself that too when the front door slams, to relax, because straining at the rope is only making it tighter, pulling her legs and arms further apart. And she's afraid of choking on the material in her mouth. Relax, relax, relax. It's not easy.

She hears the car start in the garage. He's really going through with it. People would say she asked for it, she literally asked for it, but she asked for it to stop too, and it didn't. Everything, she thinks, once I get out of this, everything is over between us.

When ten minutes have gone by and she can hear the engine still running in the garage, she begins to struggle again, desperately.

19

White Shadow

That whole time like a series of snapshots. Like the ones you'll show to your family and friends if ever you get home. Like the ones you don't have of Aborigines.

You can hear them asking, always asking, where are the Aborigines in your pictures? There you were in the outback for six months and you don't have a single Aborigine to show for it. What are they looking for, some proof that you really were where you claim to have been? Then again, sometimes you wonder yourself.

So then you'll joke - maybe you'll joke - well, in fact, there *were* some in this one, when I took it. Here, look, under this tree: a family group was gathered there. But no more. Weird, isn't it, they're gone, disappeared like ghosts from the prints, you can just make out these fleeting images, like the half-seen people in a painting by McTaggart. And on the negatives, too - see? These shadows of white. Strange, don't you think? The Vanishing Australian.

Of course, some wag might say, some worldy-wise uncle-man, they don't like you taking their photographs, do they? Think you'll capture their souls in your little black box. They don't understand, that's all. They just don't understand.

Once (you'll not say) there was this old woman in Alice Springs, ragged and stinking of alcohol. The drink had taken all sense from her voice, but she gestured at you, begging you to capture her soul for five dollars. *Take me home to your family for the price of a bottle of wine.* You turned from her and she sank back onto the empty bed of the river (it was the dry season) where she lay with others of her people. Your heart was a stone.

Later, passing by the same place, you saw her again, arguing with a white woman in shades and an "I Climbed Ayers Rock" tee-shirt. Round the white woman's neck was several hundred dollars worth of camera. "Two," she said, her voice as undiminished as if she were complaining in her local supermarket. "Two dollars only. I'm not paying five dollars for one photograph." She won her haggle, the free market setting the new price for a black woman's soul. But you have nothing to be smug about. Maybe you didn't buy the tee-shirt and you hung onto your five bucks but if you saved anybody's pride it wasn't the old woman's.

That whole time out there like an album full of photographs, to be flicked through in later life, episodes remembered, moments, sensations, but hardly ever the sequence, the chain that links them, if it ever existed. Sometimes it seems the past has no narrative: all those river metaphors for life - the bubbling burn of youth down to the estuary of old age - seem so wrong; the past is a huge expanse of still water, dotted with unreachable islands. You're like Joni Mitchell's *Black Crow* - how are you ever going to know your home when you see it again? That's what it's all about really. Knowing your place when you're at it. Knowing when to stop.

All snapshots. Through the windscreen of the Landrover the headlights pick out the weird shapes of kangaroos, frozen for a moment in the glare, then leaping into the outer darkness. "Big reds," says Pete. "Make a real mess of your motor without the roo bar." The Landrover rattles and shakes along the corrugated red dirt road, the lights dancing into the dark ahead. Pete's a loner, somewhere in his forties, gaunt and burnt and creased by the years, been through the mill and come out clean on the other side, so he says. Worked for ten years in a Brisbane factory, got married and divorced, then one day he cut loose for the dry and dusty open air. Been round the country - the continent - three times since then, picked tobacco, cotton, grapes, peaches, pears, lemons, apples, worked on a prawn-trawler, down mines, on sheep stations, cattle stations, on the roads. "I'll turn my hand to anything, mate," he says, "but I'll never go back to the city. I've been through the mill once. I feel like a caged animal whenever I get near suburbs." A bit of a player to the myth, Pete, the Man from Snowy River and Clancy of the Overflow and Joe Wilson's Mates all rolled into one - and maybe, one day, he'd get to play the old Jimmy Woodser, single and solitary in a bar, head full of myth and memory.

On the outskirts of town other shapes loom briefly in the lights. White mud streaked on black bodies. The Landrover swerves to one side. "Get out the fucking road you black bastards." This is said, not shouted, a matter of fact. "Like fucking kids," he says. 'That's a sacred site, you wouldn't think so to look at it, they collect round it like flies round a pile of shit. Corroboree my arse. Just getting pissed up to the eyeballs." The Landrover swings across the street - suddenly the town is there - and stops outside the pub. You get out, doors slamming. "You can bet your life, any time someone stakes a claim and wants to do some drilling, some Abo's going to pop up and say it's a sacred fucking site."

"So maybe it is."

"Yea, maybe. Look, those people have been around this country so long every rise in the ground has got significance. You know, they're part of the land. Part of it. The white man doesn't think like that."

"And look at the mess we make of it." This is not your voice, it's the voice of your piss-yellow conscience.

"Yea, I'm not saying they're wrong. I'm just saying, that's why they get in the way. They're a sad people, Jock. All fucked up with drink and everything. Can't take the pace. That's why you're here, isn't it? Fucking black fella walks off the job, stupid bastard didn't even pick up his wages. They're *doomed*, mate. A doomed fucking people."

The job. You tracked it down in Perth, in about the thirtieth mining company's office you visited. Four hundred miles east and north. A big lease on a sheep station where some lucky bastard had discovered a single deposit of gold worth half a million dollars. The company was test-drilling across a hundred square kilometres to see if they could find any more - or, if not gold, anything else worth extracting - copper, lead, zinc. There was a big Schramm drill-rig there on contract, and a geologist overseeing the work. Pete was the other field-assistant. You took turns by the day working with the drill, and on the off-days doing other jobs - pegging out the next lot of drill-holes, or collecting rock and soil samples from the walls of costeans gouged across the land by a digger. The costeans were scars a hundred metres long and maybe four metres deep, cruel on the flat red earth. When you were working at the bottom of one, alone in the red scar with the sky piercing blue above you, it was like being in the loneliest place in the world. This day they forgot you were out there till it was almost dark, then just when you were wondering if you could stay warm in the costean all night, Pete turns up in the Landrover. "Fucking Pearson, never told me to pick you up, sorry, mate."

Pearson - the geologist. Fastidious wee man, spent his time looking at maps and sheets of calculations, picking up rocks off the ground and putting them back again, making long phone-calls from the town to Perth. He used to hang around the Schramm, the big reverse circulation rig, looking important as he watched Stan the driller sink fifty metres of rod, standing in the way of your run from the cylinder that gathered the sample as it came up from the bore, your run to the splitter, you tipping the trays of soil into linen bags, dropping in a numbered ticket, tight with the drawstrings and tie them, then back round Pearson to the cylinder for the next sample, one for every metre, the driller's offsider maybe lending a hand when he wasn't swinging the next rod up onto the rig, Pearson still standing there making you jouk around him and waste time. And time was precious to the drill-boys, they were on contract and got paid by every metre they sank, meanwhile you trying to keep the log-book straight for the laboratory in Kalgoorlie that analysed all the samples. Then Pearson would be off to irritate Stan the Man at the gears of his drill, and get in the way of the offsider running round with the next rod and nearly cause an accident in his khaki shorts with their creases ironed up to a perfect upside-down V at the arsehole - till one day Tank the water-truck driver makes a half-run at him like an angry bull and yells, "Get the fuckahtavit, ya fucking cunt!" and that was the last seen of Pearson at the rig for a week.

Tank. "Right, Jock, get some fucking work done now, eh?" Tank called Tank because he drove the water-truck - the water to lubricate the rods going down, down into the earth - and because he was built like one. And back into the rhythm, almost like a ballad, or a mantra, *cylinder to splitter, splitter to sample, sample to bag, cylinder to splitter*, and sometimes it would be like you were outside of yourself looking down, watching your body in its endless routine in the endless bush, good working with these guys, hard, decent, crooked bastards out for themselves and their mates. You were one of their mates. Stan the Man, and Tank, and toothless Tom the mechanic - always having to sort the compressor, strip the bastard - Joe the offsider, Pete, and you - Jock was what they called you, should have worn a kilt, you could forget your own name in a place like this. Mates. Not Pearson. Fat wee Pearson, out of his safety zone, missing his wife and kids in Perth, his two kids whose photographs were printed onto his white tee-shirt, his wee breasts cupped by his children's faces, distorting their mouths. Fucking wanker.

Outside the pub, sprawled in the shadows against the wall, two or three Aborigines wrecked with drink. Vague noises mouthed at you as you pass. Pete half-turns, peers into the dark, then kicks the foot of one of them. "Hey, Neil, mate, what you doing down there?" One of the figures struggles to rise: "'Lo, mate." Pete kicks him again: "That's some state you're in." Inside, at the bar, he says, "That's the bloke that had your job. Poor bastard. He won't get another one in a hurry."

At the bar. Linda. Serving you your beers. A crack with Pete, a smile for you. Linda of the short blonde hair, hard mouth, hard face, but soft as well, bonnie and plain at once, old and young too. You struck it rich here, that's what you think, gold or no gold, with this job and this woman. Chatted to her all night a few weeks ago between her serving drinks and you knocking them back, she took you home and now you're practically living together, hardly ever in your room upstairs in the pub, the room you're supposed to share with Pete. Linda. The older woman. Almost ten years between you, and her with a six-year-old boy, making ends meet behind the bar while you coin it in sixty hours a week on the lease, putting three hundred dollars away every week so you can travel on somewhere else. She's not daft, she knows you're not here for ever. The morning after the first night together you put your hand to her face, her hard face with the three creases running from under her ear down the left jawbone, showing her age, you ran your finger down those lines and said, "You're beautiful," and she laughed and said, "Bullshit, I'm thirty-two and stretchmarks," but you insisted, "You're beautiful to me," and now watching her at work behind the bar you think it again.

The boy, Davey. "What's Scotland like?" Always the hardest questions. Out here, in this town that was hardly a town, on the edge of a huge flat emptiness, how do you answer that? What is it, was it, like? What will it be if you go back? Colder than this, more huddled and grim, older and yet not so old, standing at some crossroads with a choice, either to start walking or hang around another few years waiting for some bus that might or might not be coming. Peopled by the sons and sisters and mothers and cousins of those thousands who left for this other life. Davey doesn't want that: he wants clans and claymores and the Loch Ness monster. Give him what he wants, you grey-faced Calvinist bastard. Sorry, Davey, I don't know.

Davey's dad. Eddie Baker, a hard case. Used to be the mechanic in the garage. Linda served him his drink too. Eddie handled it badly, always had, didn't like her working once they were married, it hurt his pride to see her work. He propped up the bar all night, watching her, getting into arguments with her, fights with anybody else. The manager told her to make a choice: Eddie or her job. She barred Eddie. He sulked at home, drinking straight from the bottle. Then he walked back in a week later and assaulted the manager. He got twelve months in Fremantle.

She's tough, Linda. Paid off Eddie's debts, works all the overtime she can get, watches over Davey like a lioness. Now she's sitting almost pretty, Davey growing, waiting on Eddie getting out. She likes you but she's not letting you into her life. Not really. This suits you.

Any night in the pub you can see Stan the Man and Tank playing doubles at pool, beating off all challengers. You and Pete team up against them every half-hour and get your thrashing, keep the drill-boys in free beer all night. Then this time you say, "Double up the bevvy on this game?", and Pete looks at you as if you're insane. "It's all right," you tell him, "I'm lucky tonight." "Dunno about luck," says Tank, 'But you've got spunk. You're no Pom anyway." "Near neighbours," you say. "Can't choose your neighbours," says Tank.

So you are lucky tonight. You knock in those balls as though your life depended on it. Stan and Tank get you back on the third game but by that time you're not caring, you're shouting drunk and thinking you're entertaining Linda with your wit, forgetting this is her job, dealing with piss-artists like you and Eddie. "You're not coming back with me tonight, that's for sure," she says. Well, fuck you, you think. Who needs it? Need some fresh air but. Head for the door for some fresh air.

Outside the temperature has dropped. A black-blue sky splashed with stars, hundreds of stars you never saw in Scotland. There's the Southern Cross, symbol of something. The stars swim. You take a few steps forward to steady your sight. Trip on a foot. "'Lo, mate." The bodies are still there. You sink down to them. "You're Neil?"

The man points a long finger at you. 'Who're you, man?" "Jim," you say. But nobody knows you as that. "Jock."

"Jim Jock," he says. His mates laugh. Something is said. "Jim Jock," one of them says again. "Jim Jim." 'What?" you say, wondering as you speak how it is possible to slur a word like "what". "It's a place, man. 'S a joke. Jim Jim."

"You the Scotsman," says Neil. He reaches out and grabs your arm, pulling you into them. He smells very strong. So do you. There is the sound of liquid swilling in a bottle. Eyes upon you. You lean back against the wall. "What you doing here, man?" says Neil.

"I'm working on the lease," you say. 'Working for Bondy." But he shakes his head, "No, no, what you doing *here*, man? *Here*."

"Need some fresh air," you tell them. More laughter. A scraping noise as one of the others tries to stand up.

A bottle is thrust at you. "You're a Scotsman. Need a fucking drink, eh? Always need a fucking drink." You take the bottle. It is warm, foul, cheap wine. The second mouthful tastes better.

There is the sound of piss on wood. Protests. The one on his feet staggers a few feet further away. When he's finished he stays standing, leaning against nothing. He goes, "You wear a skirt, mate? Wear a skirt?" He goes naa-naa-na-na-naa through his nose, bagpiping to his own wild dance-steps. Then he falls over, giggling.

You're all laughing now. The bottle goes round again. A heap of you under the starry sky:

"Under the wide and starry sky
Dig the grave and let me lie . . ."

Really bevvied now. Probably time for another game of pool. Another round with the boys. Your shout. So much for fresh air. "What you doing in there with them?" says Neil. "Them bastards." "Got to play pool," you say. "Fuck pool," says Neil. "You one of us now, eh? You one of us Jock." He grips your arm again. "Got to go, mate," you say. You pull away from him and get as far as your knees. Puking in the street, the boys laughing, you laughing too, it's a fucking disgrace.

Later it's Pete getting you on your feet, "Come on, you drunken bastard, wake up!" There are skelfs in your bum and a head on you like a rifle-range. He hauls you through the door and up the stairs. But you're on your own. The others have disappeared. What happened? "Where're the boys?" you ask him. "Stan and Tank?" he says. "They went back to their camp an hour ago." "No, the boys, the boys," you say, but he doesn't seem to understand.

They locked them up, didn't they? Clear away the black trash, leave the white trash to rot or find its own way home. Put them in the cooler to sober up, what more can you do, you can't teach them any different, white fella's punished by his own guilty conscience, or gets it from the wife, black fella just goes out and does it again. It's not a problem, really. It's just how it is. Black and white. Simple.

The next Sunday, Linda has the day off too. "Let's do something with it. Let's go bush. We'll take the road out to the Cunninghame Downs station - there's an old gold town out there we can show you. I haven't been there for years." By "we" she means Davey and her, but Davey doesn't want to come, it's stupid, he says, driving for miles into the bush just for a barbecue you can have in your own back yard. He wants to stay with his Gran. You know what this is: he resents you playing mamas and papas with his mum. Fuck off back to boring old Scotland, he's thinking. My dad would show you.

It's about a fifty-mile drive. They set off in her old Holden at eleven, the boot loaded with beer in the eskie, a couple of steaks, sausages and the like, and a big pan black with charcoal. You think of the bother of building a fire and cooking the food, and wonder if Davey might not be right after all. What the hell, you're on your way.

The road is the roughest you've ever been on, a streak of red dust with bumps like a rucked up carpet and huge potholes: it only serves a couple of stations; half a day's rain every couple of months plays havoc with it. The Holden is built for it though, big and basic, the suspension given out years ago. Linda's theory is that the faster you go the less you notice the bumps, you just sail over the top of them, so she keeps her foot flat on the floor. Nice theory.

"If you follow this road right through," she yells above the racket, "you come out near Ayers Rock. Wanna go?" It's about a thousand miles of desert to Ayers Rock. "Done it already," you say. "All right, smart-ass," she says. "Well, it's only a bloody rock. I've seen enough pictures of it to last me a lifetime."

Without warning she swings off the road onto an even rougher track. You bounce along another four or five miles, conversation prohibited by the rattle and thump of the car and the clouds of dust pouring through the broken air-conditioning. Finally the track peters out entirely and you roll into an expanse of open ground devoid of the stubs of trees that cover the rest of the land hereabouts. "This is it," says Linda, switching off and letting the Holden coast to a standstill. "This is the place."

A place or non-place. Non-places and once-places are important in this vastness. This was a town, but there are no signs of human habitation, except for the lack of vegetation and a few heaps of ancient broken bottles. No graves, no wreckage of buildings, no markings where streets once ran: only the bottles, and, off in the distance, some shallow scratchings and deeper shafts where the gold-strike was.

"There was a thousand people living here once," says Linda. "Four pubs and a brothel. That's more than twice the size of our place. All gone, all gone."

You wander over the area, kicking at the dust as if it might reveal something, a secret or a nugget. Complete silence. "I love this," she says. "I don't know why. There's nothing here but I love it. I wish Davey'd come." The car is half a mile away now, a shimmering blue box in the midday heat. Not the hottest of days, but the temperature up in the low thirties and not a breath of wind.

These people that came out here in the first place. How did they know to come? That road, first beaten out by the pioneers eighty years before, with their picks and shovels and mules and bloody-mindedness. Amazing, their willingness to sweat and fight and half-die of thirst and break their backs out here for a handful of dust. All their dreams in a handful of dust.

"Gold smells," says Linda. "Even today, there are people like that - you know, you see them coming into town, real loners - they spend their whole lives sniffing, knowing it's around here somewhere. Like a dog after a bone."

You gather some wood from the stunted trees growing at the edge of the old site. The trees are not dead, but you would hardly know, they're so dry and brittle, the branches snap off like twigs, the twigs crumble in your fingers. Heading back to the car, Linda puts down her bundle of wood and points. A hundred yards off, a pair of big red kangaroos, unaware of your presence, move in lazy half-hops. You stand absolutely still, wondering how close they'll get before sensing danger. But Linda can't wait. She claps her hands and yells. They take off at once in enormous graceful bounds. You're annoyed. "What did you do that for?" She says, "I love to see them run. They're such beauties - look at them go!"

You get the fire roaring - it isn't much of a task - and pile the wood on to build up a good bed of embers. You move away from the double-heat while the flames burn down, sweeping a patch of the hard-packed ground clear of burrs and binndies before sitting down cross-legged and getting stuck into the beers.

You know now why you are here. Why she has brought you here. This is a rite of some kind. She flattens out a place in the fire for the pan, and the steaks go in with a sizzle, but all that is superfluous. She says:

"Eddie gets out next month."

"Is he coming back?"

"He'll come back."

"You'll take him?"

"For Davey. Davey needs his father."

You could say in reply, "Davey needs *a* father," but you don't want to risk it. You say, "You're telling me to go."

She doesn't answer, so you ask it another way: "Do you want me to go?"

"It's not my choice, is it?" she says. "I don't want you to go, but you're going to go sooner or later, aren't you?"

There's nothing more to be said, really. Funny how something so simple can be so hard. You both sit like stone, watching the unwanted food cook and the flames die.

"She giving you a hard time, mate?" asks Pete. A few weeks later. Ever since then, in the pub, she hardly looks at you. You shrug. "No, it's all right. I'm leaving anyway. Gave Pearson my notice today."

"Yea, I heard. Good on you, mate. Listen, do yourself a favour, get it out of your system. When you finish up, get yourself down to Kalgoorlie for the weekend, find yourself a nice young girl on Hay Street, takes your money asks no questions. Makes no demands, which is the same thing. You can get a bit of dark there if you fancy it, no trouble from the tribal elders, just make sure you use a sheath, that's all....

"Bloke I heard of, works up at Teutonic Bore, three weeks on, one week off, you know? Young bloke earning more money than he's ever seen in his fucking life before. Turned his fucking head, I reckon. He's got a girl in Kalgoorlie, he's struck on her, gives her all his money, buys her clothes and jewellery and stuff, and she takes it, by God she takes it. She's no mug, she's getting it while it's going. The three weeks he's back at the Bore, she talks about him to the other blokes she sees. Fucking thousands, he's given her. They go back and tell him, try to talk sense to him, but he won't listen. She's got him hooked around her little hooker's finger. Pretty fucking smart for a sixteen-year-old whore, eh?"

"Sixteen?"

"Well, that's what the other fellows say. She's not much more than that anyway. Old enough to bleed, old enough to butcher, that's what they say.

"Anyway, you get Linda out of your system. I might make a move in there myself if Eddie doesn't show up. Remember the three Fs, mate, that's my motto. Find 'em, fuck 'em, and forget 'em. Stick to the three Fs and you won't go far wrong."

Saturday morning. Up in the dawn with your rucksack

packed again. No fond farewells from Linda, just a hangover from a last night out with Pete and the drillers. Heading for wherever's next. At the back of your mind there's a snapshot of a grey town under green trees, dripping wet but the sun beginning to break through. Time you were there, maybe.

You walk towards the end of the street, hoping to hitch a lift to Kalgoorlie or even Perth from someone at the garage. The rest of the town is still asleep.

The sound of a Landrover coming down the street behind you makes you turn. The police heading back to their little station with the night's catch. You watch them pass, they glance at you, hardly slowing.

In the cage at the back there is a man. He grips the wire with both hands, arms stretched across the cage. There is blood on his head. You don't recognise him because when you knew him it was dark and you were drunk. Not that you know him at all.

"Hey!" he shouts. "Hey, Jock! Hey, Jim Jock!" He is laughing and shouting.

You stop in your tracks. Ludicrously, your hand rises to wave to him going by.

The Landrover lurches to the left as it turns into the police station. The figure in the back is thrown against the side of the cage, but in the half-light it seems to you like a double-image, the crucifix figure still upright, laughing at you, falling as well. And even though the vehicle is out of sight now, you can still hear the voice calling you:
"Hey, Jock! Jock! You still one of us, eh? You still one of us!"